Last Summer in Soho

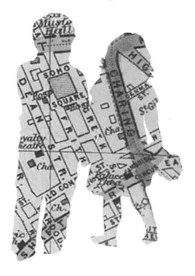

Jessica Streeting

Editor, *Penny Hosie*
Cover Design, *Nikki Wellspring*

Last Summer in Soho
by
Jessica Streeting

All characters and events in this publication are fictitious and any resemblance to real persons, living or dead, is coincidental.

For Mum, who loved this book and Nana, the school nurse who inspired us.

Table of Contents

Preface

'Write it down for me.'

I laugh.

'Would you want to read it?'

'I would! Lots of people would. It's a world that needs to be captured...'.

And a world that slips away, into the sea, as soon as I am back here. How to describe London lives, the gracious children and their ways? How to connect one life with another? This has always been the problem.

I think of Theo, the therapist's, simple summary:

'Becoming fully embodied, with all the aspects of life fitting together is as though you left something behind; your packed lunch, say. You are going back to collect the sandwich you left behind. That simple.'

I look into my friend Finn's lovely face. I marvel again that women can be granted so many loves. We sit here in funny old seaside town of Cromer, greedily grabbing precious minutes together, ignoring a gravitational pull back to home demands and responsibilities. We are middle-aged mums now, no pretending. Fully embodied? We have passed through stages and loves along the way, made babies and grown them up and now, miraculously, there is even a little time for each other. Never enough time, but some, as we sit in the pier café, looking out to sea. I remember us wedged together in the back of our parents' cars, all awkwardness and hormones, with three other girls, her art portfolio and my cello, thirty-five years back, before any of it. Now, she is planning a café of her own.

'The North Wind Community Pavilion Arts Café is quite a mouthful isn't it, Sylvie?'

'How about just The Pavilion?'

'Maybe.' Finn frowns for a second, swallowing her own mouthful of cake. 'Pavilion Arts Café?'

'P.A.C… Hmmm. Dunno.'

'But the café is becoming a reality, not just a dream, that's the wonderful thing.'

'I know.' Her eyes are shining, like we say a child's shine, over her fisherman's mug.

'I see the café as a refuge, Sylvie, a place to rest our hopes. It won't be in competition with the pier café, because that meets another need. They will compliment each other, I'm hoping.'

'One of the Soho cafés I frequent describes itself as "a haven for the convivial".'

'Such a good phrase. How about you write up your London world alongside work this term, keeping our parallel efforts to get the café up and running in mind, as inspiration. Then come and finish off in the summer holidays, keeping us open by buying our coffee and eating our cake. There, brilliant plan. Simple.'

'You'll be open, of course and ready for business.'

'Of course!'

'It would be hard for me to write a book alongside the working day…'.

'You said that brilliant psychiatrist with the funny name writes a book in a month.'

'Arty Slimreed?'

'Truly her name?'

'Yes, but I'm not a brilliant psychiatrist.'

'Imagine you are.'

I shake my head.

'Not a brilliant psychiatrist, but I suppose school nursing and that unusual lived world begs to be written about, somehow. I feel proud to be one of its number. It's hard to explain, but…'.

'Write it up, write it down, Sylvie. Tell the story of school nursing, the real story. Tell it as though you were telling me.'

'Sounds easy put like that. Meanwhile you, Finn, will win the council round with your boundless beauty, wit and charm, so that North Wind Café… or whatever you decide to call it… becomes more famous than Cromer crabs. Simple.'

Finn and I are adept at advising each other, less good at advancing our own aspirations. We are also both hopeless at making money and usually end up doing everything at a loss. This is one of the reasons I have not progressed in NHS management, though the NHS seems to do well enough at making a loss without my help. But today we're emboldened, maybe a hint of spring on the breeze. She grins.

'Deal?'

'Deal.'

Chapter One

'So, let me get this right; this term we are down to me, my student and help from Molly and Grace one day a week, if their schedules allow?'

'Put like that, yes.'

'For twenty primary schools and two secondary?'

'And Admin Olly, shared with the health visitors.'

'Olly, yes of course'

'Who's lovely.'

'Agreed. Olly is lovely. We all are, but it's not much of a team is it?'

'Your student is good.'

'Alan is superb. But strictly speaking, supernumerary.'

Ricci shakes his head, rising up from his desk, packing the small brown briefcase he always carries, so minimal, so neat in comparison with my cavernous rucksack.

'Not like the glory days when you were team lead, you mean?'

'I didn't mean that. I'm done with team leading and you're much better at it than I ever was. It's just…'

I frown, struggling to articulate just what it is, though silk purse and sow's ear hover unsaid.

'You see why we needed you back from your holibobs, Sylvie. I must be off; I'm interviewing all afternoon.'

'School nurses?'

'Nah, all health visitors, I'm afraid. You guys just aren't coming forward. Don't know why.'

'Perhaps that's because we haven't had a massive investment to the tune of four thousand extra places, or perhaps because all the money goes to the children aged nought to five…'.

Ricci squints mischievously, a single shaft of sun directly in his eyes.

'Oh, there is no money now. No money left in the pot, Sylvie dear. This basement! Natural light for one clear minute each lunchtime and the rest of the day we're in the gutter! It used to be the mortuary, you know.'

'Appropriate.'

'Ghosts galore. You can open the door here, by the way…'

He demonstrates. '… and stand outside, here, you see, under the pavement, a basement casement, to get mobile phone reception! Salubrious Soho. The heavenly Stephen Fry and some other actors whose names I forget are doing their thespian best to save this dying world you know.'

'To save our office?'

'To save Soho, my love, keep up! Theatre, art and originality, all here. There's a petition going round you know. Have you signed? Marvellous stuff.'

He shoots back in, shaking a cobweb off his beard.

'Our world may be past saving, although Early Years may yet be our salvation. Get in early. All the research concurs: Frank Field, The Marmite Review . . .'

'Marmot!'

'Yes, of course, Professor Michael Marmot. You know all this. You're the public health queen, Sylvie.'

'And after Early Years? When the babes are five and rising? Do we just write them off? Do the commissioners even care?'

'I know, I *know* Sylvie. Don't forget my doctorate is in sexual health. I'm not all babes and toddlers.'

Ricci stabs proudly at his chest, adding: "You don't have to convince me that school nurses are important. You nurture the next generation.'

'I'm sorry, Ricci. It's just…'.

'Look, we may be in the dying days of community nursing as we know it, but we can have some fun along the way, can't we? I'm retiring next year and in the meantime we should enjoy what we can. Do what we do well, together despite the crazy cuts. No?'

'You're too young to retire.'

Ricci shrugs.

'Life's too short, other fish to fry, other clichés to embody….'

He beams at me. I'm still frowning.

'It's just…'.

'Thanks for coming in when it's still your holiday - you school nurses get great holidays, you must admit.'

'Often unpaid!'

'Was your's good? You mentioned a friend with a beach café aspiration. How is that going? I might run a little café when I retire to Ireland. Or then again, I might just drift off to Mallorca and sit in the sun like a gecko. Or are they nocturnal creatures?'

13

'She's having wrangles with the town officials. It may be some time.'

Ricci doesn't seem to listen, but he takes things in, differently. It may be his dyslexic brain. I don't expect a straight conversational line.

'Important to sort things out before the others start back and the office fills up again. And let's meet for an early coffee in Soho Joe's on Monday, Sylvie. You must admit it's heaven being here in the heart of London life, despite our shitty little basement. A sort of heaven, no?'

'Okay...'. I'm thawing now, because it is impossible to be gloomy or earnest for long with Ricci.

'It's good, Ricci, you're right. This premises is right at the heart of our health community, but it's also in the coolest place in the world, after Cromer Norfolk, of course.'

'Cromer is the coldest place in the world. Perhaps we could all come and stay one weekend?'

'You'd be so welcome. And I'm sorry. You are right. Being here is so much better than the depressing offices off Edgware Road. Thank you, Ricci. And sorry to moan.'

'No worries, as the young are wont to say. Seriously Sylvie love, don't get stressed about it all. There is no point. We are NHS workers, we do our best, we make eternal compromises and (not 'but' - my therapist tells me 'but' is negative word) and... we can't save the world. Have a lovely weekend, and enjoy your overgrown kids and that long-suffering man you live with, yes?'

'He's growing a beard.'

'Good for him. Is it as glorious as mine?'

'I'm not sure it suits him. Ricci – do you feel anxious? An undercurrent of... I don't know, foreboding, or something...?'.

'The NHS is dying, Sylvie. Slowly and painfully. Of course I feel it. Take the money and look to the sunset, eh? Will you retire to Cromer eventually?'

'Well the flat in Westminster is completely a "tied cottage". We are there because of his job, so Cromer is home.'

Ricci shudders

'Far flung and Northern.'

'Norfolk is not really The North…'

'But just as well you have that bolt hole. You work in schools all day, then you live above one. Funny old life, you lead. Now Sylvie, if things get really tight here, the Powers That Be have informed me that we can always call on, you know, old whatshername from the Chelsea team…'

'Her?'

'Yes, her. I know she's dreadful, but she's experienced.' He sees my face. 'Sorry. Bad idea. Not her then. I'm off.'

Ricci makes me grin, you can't not. From the door he swings back, his curly brown hair framed by the sunbeam, a spirited faun.

'Just a thought Sylvie, but have you ever been to see Theo, the counsellor in Occupational Health? He is genius.'

'I know Theo.'

'You do? Gorgeous, isn't he?'

'Go Dr Ricci Jones. Basta! You'll be late.'

'You know Italian! Did I mention I am half Italian?.'

'Yes, you mentioned. And half Irish.'

'Yes! How clever of you to remember. I go, byeee.'

I sigh. One hour back at work and here I am, sighing again. I haven't sighed all Easter. On the surface, our holiday had been easy days; term-time cares blown out to sea, our children piling in and out of the house with their late adolescence ways, assembling doubled, sometimes tripled in number by their friends, most mealtimes. We are a cliché of a reconstituted, rambling modern family. There are other ways to live, but this has been mine, as it turned out, by accident or design. Largely, I love it, though it doesn't leave much room for contemplation.

The thing is, I shouldn't be sighing like this already because I love this too, or have done; the school nursing days, the grubby, gritty town times, the mystery of each school day. School nursing is an underrated, misunderstood profession, but those of us who 'get it', care with a passion and strive to explain to anyone who will listen.

How had the Easter break been for the London school children whose lives consume us during term time? There is a false cut-away, as though they go off set, or we do perhaps, in the holiday. The head teacher of our local boys' secondary cautioned us before Easter:

'Never tell them how much you are looking forward to your holiday. They may feel it as rejection; you preferring school to them. And never assume their holiday will be picnics and ginger beer.'

Assume nothing. A good motto for us all, really.

That head teacher had gone on to wish her staff the best of rests and endless fun times. Her advice to the children was conveyed with a catch in her throat that caught me too, listening in from the back of the tatty old sports hall.

'Stay safe, take care of each other.'

I wonder if they have. There have been several London gang attacks reported on the news this April. Half-listening from the seaside refuge,

16

each one brought a stab of unease, an ignoble hope that it's not a known child You get proprietorial over your own schools and have to mentally correct yourself - of course every child matters, wherever they are. But it gets hot and dangerous in the city. The children are not always equal to the task of safeguarding themselves.

I hover over my new desk by the fire-escape door. It won't be my desk for long, whatever Ricci promises. It will be a 'hot desk', necessarily, like all NHS space. There was a 'hot phone' when I was training at St Thomas's. President Reagan was in London and we had a 'hot phone' which, should he have fallen ill on his visit, would ring straight through to The White House. That was a red hot phone, aptly named. This desk doesn't look hot, or up to much at all, but when the President visits London later in the month, I doubt anyone will be hot-phoning this basement. An unprepossessing space, for a 'non-emergency service provider', but I like the door to the gutter and the gloaming. I don't plan to be sitting here much anyway. Eighty per cent of time in schools, maximum twenty in the office is the mantra we drill into our students, in our aim to provide a visible, accessible and confidential service.

I limit myself to a quick look at the Accident and Emergency notifications that have come through. Just a glance, not to linger here, with one foot still in holiday time, but just to prepare…

There is plenty of mishap, but nothing too worrying at first glance. Holidays can also be dull and stilted in a city. Interminable, if resources are low.

A few familiar names pop up and one ten-year-old boy has, by paramedic account bounced out of his bedroom window, passed through a restaurant awning and arrived on the table of some restaurant diners below. The name - Ali Oppah of Berwick Street, Soho.

Ali has caused a flurry of red flagged safeguarding emails. I make a note in the electronic diary to contact his school next week. Must go, time to go…

17

'Hi Mum, is it chicken, rice and pea again? I don't mind cooking it?'

I move to stand out of the gutter-well and text back, but there's no phone reception, despite Ricci's tip. Home. My half-fledged chicks are pulling me home, I think, fondly. The meal repertoire a little tired, granted, but chicken cooked in its own juices, a lemon stuck up it, lots of rice stirred in, with some peas for your five-a-day – delicious and sophisticated enough?

Hey Mum, acronym of chicken, rice and pea – CRAP – funny!

Okay, terrible meal.

Chapter Two

The head teacher of this school, a beautiful, long-limbed, unlikely person is performing her Pilates stretches by her bicycle when I puff up.

'Morning Sylvie. Another term begins.'

She adjusts her hijab. Her face exudes calm. Mine is red already.

'You look lovely, Alice. Good rest?'

'Yes, thank you. Yoga retreat in Slovenia. Doctoral thesis.'

Everyone seems to have a doctorate these days, I'm noticing, but they are very hard work to achieve, I gather.

'I wish I could do that with my legs. Thesis in…?'

'Medieval mystics. I'm comparing the Christian with Islamic'.

'Is yoga compatible with your… tradition, culture. With Islam, I mean?'

She brings her leg down in a measured, graceful way.

'Even my name is not compatible with my tradition, Sylvie. But there is much overlap in contemplative life. All religions and none.'

Contemplation.

A concept we have lost, Theo? Theo's voice often pops into my head these days.

One we make no space for, perhaps…

'Sylvie?'

'Oh, sorry Alice, yes. I was dreaming; Islam, Christianity, overlap.'

'Quite. On a more contemporary note, we have an increasing number of eating disorders and self-harming in the girls, Sylvie. Looking to address this holistically this term and beyond, with senior management. Can we count on your input, within the integral team?'

'Of course. I've audited informally with my safeguarding supervisor and along with low mood, these are what students are most frequently presenting with.'

'Just in our school?' Alice is all attention

'No, no. everywhere really. Not so much at primary school, but in Years 8 and above. Any time from twelve onwards, I think.'

'Hmm. And the other big issue for us is smooth transition. Some of our year 7's have a terrible time, I am aware of that. Something goes wrong between the halcyon days of leaving primary school, to arriving with us in September.'

'Puberty?'

'It's before that, almost, is it not?'

She gazes thoughtfully into the middle distance, drawing herself up to continue;

'And breathe in, breathe out….before the visible signs, you know? Everything is going on, under the surface. And research is beginning to suggest that some children experience that as far more traumatic than we hitherto realised.'

She is right, of course. I try to catch her calm; breathing in, breathing out….into my head pops Pearl, an eleven-year-old at one of my primary schools who is experiencing panic and shyness that have everyone baffled, not least herself. She is due to come to Langham Girls next term. Perhaps I should mention her? Alice drops into a squat.

'Excuse me Sylvie, inelegant, but so important for hamstrings. Let's work on all that then, this term, in the short time we have. And let's hope and pray for the girls. I went to Norwich this holiday, too. A fine city. You're from up that way, aren't you? I visited Mother Julian's beautifully atmospheric shrine in King Street. Her words are my mantra for this term.'

'All shall be well and all shall be well and...'.

'... All manner of things shall be well. Yes, though why did she have to say it three times? And come to think of it, self-harm and anorexia are not new concepts, are they? Hair shirts, stigmata, fasting, nothing new under the sun. All religions and none. So glad you're with us for another term. Namaste Sylvie.'

I'm dismissed.

'Namaste Alice.'

Alice's mention of Norwich sends me straight back to my Norfolk school days. At first glance, with their blue uniform and all girls' atmosphere, similar to this school. I have reminisced recently with Finn;

'Do you remember those days, Finn? You're frowning.'

'Well, we never flourished there. We were unappreciated, our copious talents completely unrecognised. And Langham girls' blue is different. Our school blue was dreary. Hadn't you noticed that Sylvie?'

'It wasn't really the thing then to recognise talents, was it? We did a lot of music.'

' We did. Tirelessly. We practiced our instruments in those small airless rooms, which was useful in the long run, but everything else was fucking awful. And thinking about it, there wasn't even any hint

21

of a school nurse Sylvie, was there? I don't remember anyone. That fierce PE teacher if you got a period pain. No one to turn to if life was strange, bewildering or just plain crap. Maybe that's why you are a school nurse now?'

'Maybe.'

Traipsing with my cello from school to Norwich station after orchestra I would pass Mother Julian's shrine. Taking deliberate detours into neglected streets that our own head mistress informed us had been bustling in medieval times, the heart of the city by the river's main thoroughfare. Edgy and dilapidated in 1983, these Norwich streets had appealed to a disengaged teen who felt herself to be at odds with the world. An anchorite cell offered a curious, if extreme solution to life's complexities. Celibacy was not immediately attractive as a prospect, but since the mystery and joy of sex eluded me entirely at that time, I didn't dwell on that aspect. Rather, the difference, the setting apart, the deliberate disassociation from the world and its ways. Mother Julian had been 'Called', which sorted out the problem of what to do with one's life. On a pragmatic level, escape from the plague and pestilence of medieval Norwich made complete sense. And had Mother Julian been what we would now call anorexic, or just aesthetically frugal? Our headmistress informed us that Julian existed on berries and bread, poked through her priestess cell window by faithful parishioners and the love of Our Lord, manifest in visions.

***

'Sidney Carter wrote our next hymn. He was a poet, folksong writer and pacifist, born just up the road in Camden Town, 1915, one hundred years ago, but the sentiments and the lovely tune resonate freshly today...'.

Alice is in full flow. Multi-cultural London town, first day of the summer term and here they all are, five hundred students and staff crammed into the adjoining parish church for the first morning of term. No one seems to be listening much, though maybe they take it all in, like Ricci, differently. But the girls at this parish school sing, unusual for London. They rejoice in singing loudly and lustily, in fact they do everything demonstrably here in that best spirit of girls who feel free, without boys around. And Finn is right, their uniform is an extraordinary blue, full of light and summer sky. There are several reedy young men dotted round the church with their year groups and a natural sprinkling of senior male teachers, but predominantly this is a place where girls feel free to be adolescent girls and that means raucous, inelegant and fun, indomitable and formidable. If the Victoria Boys' could see that this is how girls can present en masse, they might be surprised, relieved even. Or terrified out of their wits. Each school a different world. This is just one.

In this central London borough, where the social demographic is splendidly diverse, there are an incongruous number of Christian-based faith schools. They date from the philanthropic Victorians, often as this one, forward thinking for its time, pre-dating the 1870 Education Act by fifty years, attached to a church, taking the name of the saint their church is dedicated to. In this congregation, lots of girls are Muslim, some are Jewish, some Christian, few overtly anything much. But the families of faith seem to prefer a faith school of any faith, to the nebulous, disbelieving absence that they perceive pervades a non-faith school.

I expect the people gathered here have mixed feelings on faith and God and love and music. Don't we all? Didn't we always? But here, everyone is singing. Sidney Carter's words may have more immediate resonance here than they did in my own Norfolk primary school days, where we embraced the ethos as enthusiastically as we shouted the tune, even though we had only one black boy in the whole school, adopted from Uganda.

'And the creed and the colour and the name won't matter, were you there?'

After today's sing song and a brief, dull announcement from me about remembering to bring back consent forms for the HPV jabs, we all file out and I slip into the little room ordained for me on Wednesdays, where I can see people for what we call One2One.

It's cold, like a little anchorite cell, but people do come. In this school, children referred to me arrive at their prescribed time and I never have to go searching. This is a well-run school where, miraculously, they seem to understand the place of the school nurse. The staff appreciate our contribution - wholly pastoral with the emphasis on health - and send all sorts our way.

Then at lunch time there is a drop-in, which basically means another place to eat your lunch and chat. Finn and I would have hung out here, if there had been one back in our Norwich school days. There is more to it all than that, if you like; a sound evidence-base for interventions of this sort, which reduce social isolation, promote resilience and help the young to navigate their own path to health. But maybe there's not so much difference between what school nurses can afford as a place to be and the old friendly art room at my school; where a person could mingle with the paint smell, high studio windows and gently disappear.

'Finn, do you remember the art room?'

'I do. Crocus Lettison in her artist's smock.'

'Was she really called Crocus? She looked like a bulb and she always had a drop on the end of her nose. Kind to us though, wasn't she? Pottering around with her oils.'

'And lino for the ones who couldn't draw. I remember all of it, but I don't remember you there, Sylvie. Art wasn't so much your... not meaning to be rude...'.

'No, fair enough, Finn. I was firmly in the lino camp... but for a while I liked the art room, as a place to be.'

24

Schools today have more places like this than when we were little. Pastoral care is better understood and embedded within the fabric of school life, so there will be learning mentors and teaching assistants and youth workers and other names for people who hold in common a genuinely 'open door'.

'Come in, tell me about yourself, or not if you'd rather. Just be.'

I unpack my bag. All you really need for a day in a school seeing individual children is some paper and coloured pens and then your undivided attention. There is a set of scales and a height measure locked in the cabinet, but they rarely come out for the first visit; with the eating disorder spectre looming large. All our notes will be electronic, waiting for our input back at the Soho hot desk. I have a little iPad for constant contact with the NHS Trust, but it's all quite minimal really, as the important aspect is time spent listening, one to one.

Also tissues. Theo has taught me to always have tissues.

Permission for tears, even if tears seem far away.

Later this term I will be teaching all this at the university linked to our Trust, to new school nurse students. I will explain to them that school nursing is not a pure discipline, like medicine, but encompasses many, so it stands to reason that our assessment process should be drawn from a box of tools.

Health and wellbeing assessment is central to our role, I will say, and that role, so hard to define, is important. We are not counsellors, though our interventions can be therapeutic. Our primary job when meeting a young person is to assess them holistically, then refer as appropriate. This may be back to someone in school, on to their GP, specific health service, or a combination of all these. A good health and wellbeing assessment takes no longer than half an hour, maybe forty minutes, but it has taken me twenty years to learn, following the example and learning of different colleagues (particularly therapists).

In one of my schools, very different from this one, but three blocks away, I share a small office with three psychotherapists, a social worker and a policeman. In that school there is minimum space but maximum understanding of the need for therapeutic support of young people within the school context: "Don't leave your baggage at the door, bring it in and let us help unburden you.'

Working within a multi-disciplinary team has influenced my assessment development hugely and that is the point of public health to me. Populations, communities, but at heart the individual. Working together, a patchwork. I have evolved an assessment tool now, which I will offer to the students from our box of tools, I will say.

I call it Still Small Voice.

I may not add that last sentence, but keep it in my head. Still Small Voice, my own name for my own assessment tool is such a small voice still, that it dare not speak its name. I will probably call it a health and wellbeing assessment tool and leave Still Small Voice to grow quietly. Or is that hiding my 'Still Small Voice' under an assessment bushel? Maybe I need to be pushier with my ideas. Nurses don't tend to foist their own creations onto people. But there is more of a place these days for entrepreneurism in nursing. Maybe…

There is a rustle at the door, not a knock, more like a tiny mouse rustling, but the door opens and a small face peeps round, determined not diffident;

'Ana!'

The whole person appears into the room, sitting down quickly as though to claim the space before anyone else can grab it.

Huge grin.

'Lovely to see you. How are you Ana? How was your holiday?'

Too many questions and she doesn't answer anyway, just smiles on, as though to let me get over my enthusiasms and calm down.

'Lipstick looking good'

She nods, grinning even wider at our private joke;

'I'm allowed to wear it in the last term.'

'That bright, even?'

'Yep.'

Ana had been referred to me the previous September, a girl who was slipping away; falling attendance, falling off the mouse wheel of learning, physically diminutive and growing smaller by the day, becoming almost literally invisible.

We had built a picture of her life together, starting as I always do now, by asking her to choose a colour from my pens. It doesn't seem to matter if they are aged five or fifteen – choosing a colour is a good start.

Ana had picked a bright ruby red.

'The same colour as your lipstick'

And the grin, exploding from a shutdown, mouse face. Transfiguring.

In the middle of the page we were building; a basic family tree, noting down what mattered to Ana, who she lived with, what school was like and so on, I had added 'RED LIPSTICK' in red. And underlined it. She saw me write it and nodded approval.

As we tried together to unwrap Ana's tightly packed bundle of worries over the year, the lipstick had become a kind of touchstone, a representation of her identity. She was too small and not eating, watching and absorbing all the angst of her intense and complicated family, until she threatened to disappear completely, but the lipstick was a way to hold on to her own self. This coupled with a quiet insistence on an oversized sweat shirt, not school uniform. Dark blue hijab, baggy school jumper, shapeless, long skirt – all good ways to hide an anorectic body. Radiant lipstick told us 'I am still here…'.

I had referred her to our mental health service and had spoken to her GP. I also talked to her father and liaised (a word we use a lot) with school incessantly. None of the interventions made much of an impression on her, but Ana kept coming along in snatched moments and in the end, her small, strong rebellions, not anything we could do or say, were her way to pull herself back to life and the rest of it.

'I don't have long, Sylvie. Have to go to maths, but I wanted to say hello.'

'So good to see you. I don't have long either, today. We are very short staffed; I am going to have to spread myself pretty thin this term.'

'Still coming on Wednesdays, though?'

I am frowning again, distracted by the staff numbers crisis, running a mental calculation that goes: 'Twenty schools, two school nurses… and falter. If we don't spend a minimum whole day at each secondary school, how can we be the 'visible, accessible, confidential service' young people have said they need?

They hold us to a regular time and place, because that is what they need. The very least they deserve.

'Yes. Still Wednesdays.'

'Good'.

Ana leaps up and gives me a bony, unexpected hug.

'Bye then. And book me in next week for a proper catch up? I can't miss any core subject or geography though, so…… period three, after break?'

'Period three next week, straight into the diary then.'

'Thanks'

The grin.

Gone.

How are we going to manage this crisis? School nursing numbers have been bad before, but never this lamentable.

Your job is un-doable. There is a reason you are becoming extinct.

Thanks for that, Theo.

Just putting it out there. And you invest too much erotic energy in it all.

I do not!

Ana is not the only one with identity issues. In school nursing we are hideously conflicted; we have a sticky history of employing unqualified school nurses who have not passed the specialist degree, but are general nurses employed at base level pay. This situation evolved because we didn't ever have quite enough qualified school nurses and needed to make up numbers. Health visitors, who do the same training as us, but with more emphasis on babies and young children, don't have this problem, because you cannot be called a health visitor until you are qualified. In school nursing, we have historically approached it as though it's an easy old job that pretty much anyone, with a bit of basic nursing and a friendly manner, can do. Bonus points if you have kids of your own.

You see we do ourselves few favours.

Health visiting has recently benefitted from government investment, supported by a strong wall of evidence about the importance of early years' attachment. Despite the increasing body of literature showing us that change is possible into adolescence and that adolescence continues well into our twenties even, no more money comes school nursing's way, no grand investments.

I recently heard the Chief Nurse of England say school nurses punch well above their weight. A compliment. I like the idea of being punchy, 'up against it', whatever 'it' is, but the 'school nurses against the world' mentality will only go so far. I doodle 'SCHOOL NURSING in red capitals, then underline it. We have an identity problem that red lipstick may not solve.

Another knock at the door. And so on until lunch time, with students continuing to arrive, according to a list prepared by diligent head of years, coordinated by the safeguarding lead and overseen by the all-seeing Alice.

I meet Rejoice, a thirteen-year-old Zimbabwean refugee, who has recently moved from temporary housing in Slough to a precious, rare placement in Camden, near Tottenham Court Road. Rejoice tells me she lives with her dad, who is a gentle man. Their mum and six siblings are to join them later in the year, she hopes. Staff have concerns that she is thin, not because of an eating disorder in this instance, but because there isn't enough food at home. We talk about the food bank Rejoice and her father visit twice a week and the chemist nearby that sells cheap vitamins with iron for growing girls.

Rejoice misses her mum and the little ones, but is more keen to tell me about her life plan to run a music company specialising in Korean pop.

I see Philomena, a fifteen-year-old, who cares for her mum but makes light of it.

'Only five minutes today, Sylvie. I am very busy, but maybe I'll bring my lunch in, yeah?'

I see three more girls, each very different from one other and then it's the lunch time Drop In, when lots of the younger ones cram into the room, to shovel their lunch before rushing off to running club.

'You grow out of that caper,' says Philomena, with a worldly look.

'You don't run anymore? You used to be good.'

'No. It's for kids, playing, messing about.'

'Do you do any sport now?'

'They wanted me to run after school, competitions and that... but how can I? You know, with Mum...'

I make a note to talk to her head of year. There are ways to help. This is Philomena asking for some, as overt as she will ever be. Important to pick up the signs.

I have to leave after lunch; not a whole day today because of a necessary meeting about recruitment, but for many people in this city, a day's work is all meetings. Heading back to the office, I walk past the BBC at Langham Place, over Oxford Street and back to our stately old building in Soho Square, once a Victorian Women's hospital. This is not a sight-seeing tour of historic London town, but part of my actual job. I'm being paid to spend time here, puzzling health out and piecing things together, with each young person and their story.

Chapter Three

Letting myself into the tiled old hall, I acknowledge the ghosts. Nod to Glory, nod to Sally, with only a passing twinge of a worry for myself.

You going mental, Sylvie? Talking to dead people! Philomena would scoff if she were here.

Hope not, Philomena.

In the ten years I have worked for this NHS Trust, lots of people have come and gone, but two particular people have died. Both happened to die after I had last seen them here, in our tatty old building which has old, barely converted Nightingale wards for large meetings and teaching sessions. The nicest rooms on the first and second floors have been partitioned off now, for renting out to corporate space, though they stand empty, with the smell of new carpet. Glory, an 'old school' school nurse, who trained long before the Specialist Community Public Health Nurse degree was invented (with its awkward acronym SCPHN *'scuffen' 'scoughen' 'schiphen'*...), died suddenly one night after we had spent an afternoon together 'refreshing our competencies around' oral health. The course had been particularly good, revealing to us that nowadays we should be brushing very gently, with the softest of soft brushes, for no less than two whole minutes. Round and round, as though each tooth was a pearl of great price. We had learnt the terrifying fact that dental extraction has become the most common reason for children under ten needing general anaesthetic.

We had sat rapt, for several hours, learning about a lovely concept called therapeutic dentistry, where the dentist acknowledges fears and phobias and welcomes children and their parents in, with loving care. We chatted about how it is possible to learn something new even when you're quite old - and planned together to change our practice from henceforth. Glory had only weeks left to school-nurse. She was due to retire, had just paid off her mortgage and was looking forward to moving back to Southern Ireland.

We had said goodbye with a hug in the tatty old hall, with the lovely green tiles and high ceiling, and gone home.

'I love this staircase!' Glory stood on the bottom step, breathing in appreciatively.

Arts and Crafts, you know Sylvie, a fine example.'

'You a bit wheezy, Glor?'

'It's nothing, dear. Just my usual. I abide with asthma; asthma abides with me. Now wasn't that an interesting session?'

'Your asthma hasn't really cleared up at all this year, has it.'

'Ah, forget my asthma, it's my old teeth I'll be looking to now Sylvie. Poor little stubs, with me through thick and thin.'

She chuckled.

I guess Glory brushed her teeth with more care that evening. I did. But in the event, dental health was to be less of an ongoing concern for her, as she died of an acute exacerbation of her chronic asthma that night. I think of Glory most nights when I brush my teeth. And I always think of her when I come into our hall that time forgot. I don't smell any perfume, hear her actual voice out loud and it's not strange or scary, but there is a distinct presence to acknowledge, or absence, maybe.

33

There is something of the Persephone archetype about you, Sylvie.

Theo?

The Underworld, Hades. Never entirely far away.

Oh, right.

The other person who died was at the very top of her career; our Children's Director, five years ago now. She was one of those rare people who managed to make everyone feel valuable and that they had a particular relationship with her. This wasn't disingenuous. Everyone she met did matter to her. We were a smaller organisation then and though far from perfect, there was a feeling that with Sally at the helm we could navigate the storms and drop anchor together, sometimes.

The evening Sally died was still and mid-summery, after a Trust-wide party on Soho Square. Everyone was packing up, bringing empty Pimms bottles back into the building, folding tables, picking up our litter. I bumped into Sally coming out of the ladies, thanked her for the party, muttered something about it being great we could all get together like this. 'Sylvie,' she said, 'I'm aware that school nursing needs investment. We must talk. Come and see me next week?'

I floated home that golden evening, soft sun on Shaftesbury Avenue, feeling warm towards the organisation I belonged to, optimistic about my chosen profession and excited for our future.

But (or should I write 'and' as Ricci's therapist recommends?) Sally died that night from something that is vaguely called 'Sudden Adult Death', in her early fifties, no more. We waited for more detail, but that was all there was. It happens sometimes, as we knew because we are nurses, after all. She was among us and then she stopped being. And we were sad. There is still an abiding sadness.

Is that just me, Theo - the abiding sadness?

34

No. Others feel it. Existential sorrow for our health service, that cannot be what it was, maybe never was. Maybe it is the death of a dream?

Maybe. Do you see Ricci too, for sessions like these, Theo?

Ricci who?

The right answer.

So I think of Sally too, when I come in off the square. I nod to them, as I manoeuvre my bicycle in, or wipe my feet. Glory, Sally. I wonder who will be next and hope it won't be me and Theo suggests I dwell too much in the underworld, but it's as though the underworld comes up to meet us sometimes.

Don't cycle home in this ghost person frame of mind, Sylvie. You can't pass through buses.

No. Good tip.

Theo is inordinately helpful, practical and discreet. Happily, I am seeing him later today. The real Theo is less alarming than the one inside my head.

'Arty Slimreed says we should reveal more of our selves in our interactions with clients. Our own vulnerabilities.'

'Interesting name.'

'Isn't it? What do you think, Theo? The old school was that we didn't mention our own problems because we need to focus on the young person and put ourselves aside to better concentrate on them....'

'They won't hear what they don't need, so too much "when I was your age..." talk will be a waste of time. But your congruence comes through anyway, in your empathetic listening, your ability to hear the message behind their words. You know what it is to have been thirteen, fourteen, four…'

'I didn't always.'

'Well, you *did always*, but you were a bit disconnected from yourself. Now you are very much in tune.'

'Am I? Sometimes I feel overwhelmed.'

Theo smiles. He is so nice.

'And now you can say that you feel overwhelmed. And the world doesn't end. Arty Whatsit is right.'

'Slimreed.'

I am with Theo for 'supervision', which is really a kind of therapy of course, but I find that hard to write. All too happy to refer children and young people for counselling and art, drama or music therapy when they confide that their mood is low, yet I am barely able to voice the fact that I go along myself and talk to Theo. Though our Trust is not blameless - described by some as 'an organisation in psychosis' and if so, then only reflecting the exact state of the greater NHS – it has one great quality and that is the Occupational Health Department. The sane mind of our collective whole, the healthy part that sustains us all, from 'flu jabs to physio. And yes, if we feel a bit down, or overwhelmed, or unable to sleep, or if slipping under a bus seems suddenly appealing, then Occupational Health are there for us, too. Calm, organised, with an appointment system that works, short waiting lists and, in a small room, overlooking the Paddington Basin, Theo himself.

'Do you think he might be God?' Ricci had asked me on the bus one evening.

'Probably.'

'He is so handsome, don't you think, Sylvie? And tall.'

'Is he?'

'Yes, Sylvie.'

'Oh.'

In truth, I struggle to remember what Theo looks like, because I am so busy talking about myself when I meet him. He is a grey blur, exuding empathy and infinite wisdom. Would I even recognise him in the street? And that could be considered insulting, after all. I will make a proper effort to look at him next time.

'Yes. I think he is probably God. I sometimes hear his voice in my head.'

'Me too.'

Sally had appointed Theo shortly before she died. And so, I suppose, he and his team were her legacy.

They work with some of us, maybe they work with many of us; you don't know, because you slip along when you have space in your day or make space after or before work. You talk, or cry or laugh and they listen mindfully, so that you can go back to your patients or clients - or my case, children, their families and their schools - with the necessary detachment to help effectively, but more in touch with your own suffering and self. Compassionate and suffering with, not empty pitying.

It was through visiting Theo that I made a bit of a breakthrough with my assessment of children. Prior to that it had been hit and miss when they came in to see me, despite years of training; diving into my box of tools, pulling out what seemed relevant. Trying to listen, rather than just ask about the complaint they had been sent with, or what teachers had seen fit to see as concerns on their behalf. Knowing they were more than a label; 'acne ridden', 'young carer', 'obese', 'low attender'.

We had been puzzling through my own adolescence;

'Go away and make an assessment of yourself at thirteen, Sylvie,' he had said.

'Do what you would do for a child who comes to you. See how that looks.'

For the first time I had applied the tools of my trade to myself. I started with a gentle genogram, or family tree. I used the useful HEADSS acronym devised by Goldenring and Rosen in the 1970s as an aid to doctors struggling to get inside teenagers' heads. I asked myself questions about home, education, eating, activities, drugs, sex, sleep, safety. And I placed all of it in the context of our Common Assessment Framework triangle, which though extremely useful, can be hard to interpret on its own. How did I look aged thirteen? What would have been my professional opinion if this young person had walked through the door?

I used the smattering of solution-focused knowledge such as asking myself what, on a scale of one to ten, would be my mood. At home? At school? And then that all important question; 'what might better look like?'

Finding that hard to answer, I tried: 'If I could wave a magic wand – how might things look?'

I had plodded dutifully back to Theo with my precious scrap of paper reflecting myself at thirteen and he had held my story in mind with careful attention, with compassion, actually.

'Some of it is funny, after all.' I'd said

'Very funny.'

'And a bit sad.'

'Very sad, Sylvie.'

Together we had sat with sad and how that felt.

'I see why you have the tissues.'

'Always.'

Then my hour was up and I would cycle back off into my life again. Sometimes Theo would gently recommend that I leave my bike and walk, slowly for a while.

School nurses cannot expect to have long with a child. Sometimes we only have five minutes, or thirty, or maybe an hour. We have to accommodate the fluctuations of a school timetable. When we refer on, we are safe in the knowledge that their appointment will be as clearly boundaried as our own at Occupational Health. But we see them swiftly, at source, unencumbered by waiting lists. Every contact needs to count, so assessment needs to be effective. Since seeing Theo, I hope I've got better at using my tools effectively, but also at giving the space between the words equal weight, or more. A place to be, a space to be.

And they can't always fall straight back into school line. I certainly couldn't have, after spending time with my thirteen-year-old self, that day with Theo. It had been late afternoon in early summer. My plan had been to hurtle straight back to the office, but abandoning my bike on his instruction, I had found myself walking slowly along the canal, through Little Venice, towards Paddington, processing. And somewhere along the tow path I recognized the Norwich teenager, who had got lost along the way. And joined up with her again.

'Working with you has made me a better practitioner, Theo. You know, I like to think that very gradually, through you and your team, a new spirit grows in our flawed old organisation.

'That may be your fantasy' he says, which I interpret as modest deflection.

Today I am wanting to check out that I am not mad in acknowledging Glory and Sally…'So every morning, I greet them as I step into that Arts and Crafts, tiled hall. Do you know what I mean about that place? It's from another era.'

Theo nods enthusiastically. He seems more in focus today and I am confident that I could easily identify him in a line up parade.

'I know just what you mean. It's incongruously beautiful, with those old green tiles, elegant, almost pastoral. There will be many more ghosts in there than just Glory and Sally. You are not mad, Sylvie. You have known and loved them. You find them there in the hall. Others may too. Have you asked them? Now tell me what you've been dreaming…'.

Chapter Four

'You see its rained in here again.'

When I arrive at the boys' school, Alan my student is mopping a substantial quantity of water from the floor, the desk, and the computer.

'This really isn't good enough as a room, Alan.'

We look up at the polystyrene breeze block ceiling. There is no dripping, so it's hard to ascertain exactly where the water has come in, but this is not the first time.

'At least it is a room,' says Alan

'The kids come here because it's out of the way – they like it. Look at their art work.'

Alan proudly indicates a rash of homemade posters on the theme of Drop-in adorning the far wall;

'Great stuff. Did the Year Sevens do them?'

'It started as Year Seven, then grew to people from every year. One of them even brought this bean bag in from home, which luckily missed the rain drops. And a bowl for fruit.'

'Did you provide the fruit?'

'Yeah. It wasn't so much money. I got it from the market.'

'We should reimburse you from petty cash'.

'We don't have petty cash in school health, do we?'

'No. Sorry, we don't. Alan, you have made this place lovely. Well done.'

Alan blushes. 'It was the boys, really. There are a few referrals I'd like to go through with you, if that's okay?'

Alan is my student school nurse this year. He has flown through the year and now we are in May, has sufficient 'competencies', as we call them, to be left to work unsupervised at times. I don't like this word, I don't like reducing nursing to 'competencies'. It's my view that Alan had more competencies than me on his very first day. He came to the course already an experienced nurse with a background in adult mental health, but doing a public health degree in a year, with fifty per cent in practice is an undertaking for anyone. The course, whenever you take it, is transformative. If you have been working as a school nurse before, it makes sense of everything, gives a theoretical base to the work you have been doing naturally. If you come directly in, with this your first experience of school nursing, you learn both theory and practice together. Probably a better way around, but both have their advantages. The diversity of entrants can be a challenge for practice teachers such as me. There is no standard student

'Have you seen everyone Jean referred today?'

Alan casts his eye down the list of referrals, written in a clear hand, unbelievably neat, like an exercise for primary school children.

'There is still a year seven boy called Plank McDougal to see. He . . .'

'Plank?!'

'I know. Apparently, he is being bullied.

'Plank?!'

Yeah, you can kind of see why. I thought Alan was bad enough.'

'Alan's a perfectly fine name.'

'Yeah, kinda, but very old fashioned. I wonder if Plank's parents are from Jamaica too …Mine have a lot to answer for. I'm named after some old doctor my parents revered. Anyway, Plank hasn't come yet. What are our plans for this afternoon?'

'We need to make a home visit to Ali Oppah after school – the boy who fell out of the window, remember? But we have an hour to spare. Do you want to go and search for Plank?'

There is a clatter from the stairs outside our inadequate room and before we can speak again, a small black boy has appeared, slammed the door and pressed his back against it, noisily out of breath.

'Hello.'

We stare at the boy.

'You okay?' Alan asked gently

The boy nods, looking close to tears and wheezing dramatically.

'Running from someone?'

He nods again.

'Can we help you?'

'I'm meant to be here, innit?'

'Are you?'

'I'm Plank. They mock me for my name.'

I move to sit down by the door, as Alan leads Plank into the main body of our room, away from the large damp patch. Alan can do all this now, as though I were not here at all. Better to become almost invisible and let him practice.

They will have half an hour together; time enough for Alan to make a reasonable assessment if he asks the right questions and listens carefully. Which he will.

Alan pours Plank a glass of water. Plank eyes the fruit bowl.

'Go on, have an apple. Its fine.'

'Thanks.'

Alan introduces us, explains our role and runs through the confidentiality boundaries, which it is always good practice to do first. Then he asks Plank to choose a colour. Plank considers for a moment, before picking a bright green felt pen.

'Apples. My favourite green. Can I have another please?'

'Go ahead.'

With the green felt tip Alan makes a big square in the middle of the page.

'This square represents you, Plank.' He writes 'Plank' in the middle.

'Now, when were you born?'

Plank grins, still out of breath, but calmed by Alan's gentle presence.

Alan has studied the referral form, neatly completed in Miss Jean Keane's rounded hand. Jean is lead in this school for all things safeguarding; a protecting mother hen to the whole of Year Seven.

'I know things haven't been that easy for you at home lately, Plank. Have you recently moved?'

'We live in a hostel off Tottenham Court Road.'

'You moved there recently?'

'Yeah, before that we all lived in our house, in Camden. All my life. We fell into debt.'

Appropriately old-fashioned phrase. 'Into debt' and virtually into the workhouse, it seems.

'And "we" are?'

'I live with my mum.'

Alan draws a circle above his square and a line connecting them.

'Who is called?'

'Cynthia.'

Alan writes 'Cynthia' in the circle.

'And my dad – he's called Harold.'

Alan writes Harold in a square above and to the left, joining it to Plank's square.

'And the little ones: Angus, Sidney and Lloyd.'

Alan carefully attaches three more squares. Plank frowns at the paper, his family, his life, properly engaged now'. Without taking his eyes off the unfolding genogram he rummages in his trouser pocket and pulls out a dusty blue inhaler.

'Do you need to take that? We can stop for a minute.'

'S'okay'. Planks draws in the salbutamol, swallows, coughs, then shoves the little blue life-saver back into his pocket;

'Yep, that's right. Angus is eight, Sidney is six and Lloyd is four. There isn't much room in the hostel.'

'I bet. Do you share a room?'

'We all of us shares. Mum and Dad go in one bed, Me and Angus go in the one by the window and the little ones share the sofa bed.'

'What about cooking? Is there a kitchen?'

'One down the corridor. Mum makes us tea, while Dad takes us out to the park, because it's a bit crowded in there at tea time'

'You share the kitchen?'

Yep. With the others on the corridor. And the toilet.'

'And the bathroom?'

'Shower. Yeah.'

And in this way Alan will gently tease out the social determinants of Plank's health There is a social gradient and we are all on it, scrabbling up, sliding down. This is where Plank McDougal's family are positioned, in Central London today, which is not okay at all, of course. Professor Michael Marmot has provided us with clear data that explains this, with his work on health inequalities. Plank's parents have fallen on hard times and all this country can provide is a grotty hostel, which is only marginally better than street level at the bottom of the hill, and a poor reflection on us all. When they are housed, they will in all likelihood move out of Central London, but there may not be a school place for Plank near his home…

Alan doesn't need me here in school with him anymore. He will not neglect to ask why Plank arrived so abruptly, slamming the door behind him, puffing and teary. He will follow up the bullying that Plank will feel able to disclose, with Jean Keane, because this school (like every school) has a 'Zero tolerance' of bullying, but human children are inclined to bully. Alan will ask about Plank's cough, ascertain when the family last went to their GP for full checkups, speak to Plank's parents if possible, offer to support in any way, to liaise with the GP and so on and by the end of this afternoon, Plank's health and wellbeing will be held in the mind of those who should be able to help a very little bit.

'Alan, I'm leaving you two together. I'll visit Ali and meet you back at the clinic later.'

They both look up, as though they'd forgotten I was there anyway.

'Sure, no worries.' Alan says.

'My mum says 'no worries' an' all. But there are worries, aren't there? Big worries.'

'Sometimes worries are big,' Alan agrees. 'Do you have worries, Plank?'

Planks face is a perfect circle, his eyes innocent rounds.

'Yes. I told you. They mock me for my name.'

Plank's solemn refrain.

I slip out onto the basement corridor and up the stairs, to a flash of afternoon sun. It is always cold in Alan's insalubrious school nurse room, even when it's not 'raining'. Every year school and The Trust solemnly sign a Partnership Agreement, which states schools' obligation to provide 'a suitable room'. No windows, no sense of the day at all in this one, unless you count the unusual feature of occasional raindrops. No clock on the wall, but we measure time here by bells and the tannoy speaker system and the intermittent elephant thuds of whole year groups hammering up and down stairs.

***

'Oi, Ali, you fat pig, d'you wanna play out?'

A fierce little pale person with scraggy plaits stands in the middle of the small Peabody Building courtyard, hollering her invitation up several floors of redbrick wall.

'Oi, Ali. Aliiiiiiiiii! She pronounces 'out' this way: 'A-a-a-a-ht'.

A white boy of about ten, kicking a ball aimlessly round the flower beds, stops by her side.

'He can't, remember?'

'What?'

'Ali's not allowed to play out since his tumble, remember?'

'Oh yeah.' Says the girl. 'Forgot.'

But the two continue to stare up expectantly

'Is that where Ali Oppah lives?', I ask them.

The little girl turns, nodding and chewing her plait.

'Yeah. Fat pig Ali Oppah.'

'We call him Space Hopper,.' added the boy. Flat 401. If you're going up, can you ask him when he can play out?'

'Miss him?' I ask.

'Yeah. He's a lump, but he's funny and he's quite a fast runner. Not as fast as me.'

'None of them's allowed out now, after what happened. Not Ali, not his sisters,' said the girl

'They all play in.'

'He fell out of the window, Miss. Bounced! That's why we call him Space Ho—'

'Yes, I see.'

'Well we called him it before, so it's even funnier now. He's fat, so it's funny, get it?' You his social worker?'

'School nurse.'

'Oh yeah, thought I recognised you. You're coming in to do our sex talk soon. I'm at Piccadilly Primary, Year Six? I know. I look younger, don't I?'

Small and slight, with these yellow, tatty plaits, but not so young, when you come to look properly. Shrewd eyes.

'I haven't started my thingy, you know, yet. You said some might by the end of Year Six, but I don't think I will.'

'Everyone is different,' I say obviously.

'Ha!' She laughs suddenly and twirls round, shoving the boy, who had sat down on the step and was poking a snail with a stick. 'See. I told you I was normal.'

The boy puts his hands over his ears.

'Can you stop talking about periods, Kayleigh.'

'We've hardly started, for your information,' Kayleigh snaps back, rolling her eyes at me. 'Men!' She tosses a plait.

'I'd better go up and see Ali. I'll give him your love,' I say.

'Ga-ay!' shouts the boy.

'Best regards then, if love's not allowed.'

***

Mrs Oppah eyes me warily, holding the door half open.

'I know you from the school, and when you sent Ali to Fat Club, but you don't normally do home visits, do you?'

'Not very often, but my clinic base is only round the corner and we thought you might need a little extra support, after everything that's happened, Mrs Oppah. And it wasn't really called Fat Club.'

'I'm a terrible mother.'

'No, no. I'm sure...'.

'Oh come in, anyway. It's still quite cold out there.'

Mrs Oppah ushers me into a small, hot room, where Ali, who I do remember from our early intervention weight reduction programme, sits like an emperor on a red velour couch, one hand moving rapidly over a laptop balanced on his left arm cast, a plastered foot sticking out from under a hairy rug. The telly is on and two sisters sit, legs crossed staring at the screen. One looks over at me, then back to the telly, unquestioning.

It's not true that all children play on games all the time. Telly still has its place and this television is an old-fashioned set, square and grey. It seems that in Ali's house there is one computer and Ali commandeers it. His epic 'tumble' has afforded him prime status within this household.

Ali's mum says: 'We've had so many people round, checking up on us. I thought they were going to take Ali and the girls away. There was an emergency meeting at the hospital, but the doctor said it was obviously an accident. I think they believed her in the end. She was angry at them for wasting her time, when she had lives to save. I tried to explain . . . Ali is boisterous, the window is low, there were old bars on it, they must've been rusty or loose.'

'Ali broke them when he fell out?'

Mrs Oppah nods sorrowfully.

I had seen the notes of this emergency case conference and the swift dismissive remarks of the consultant surgeon, who had put Ali back together, in response to Children's Services' questions. She continues:

"They said I was at home neglecting Ali, but I was only in the kitchen making the kids' tea. He and the girls were fighting on the bed and he rolled out. I can show you the bedroom window, it's low, the bars were rusty, did I say? They had pushed the bed up against the window for bouncing. I didn't know. I'm a terrible mother . . . I haven't slept since.'

Mrs Oppah sits down tentatively on the edge of a hard chair next to Ali, who has stopped playing the game and is still, his eyes moving from me to his mum.

One of the sisters swings round, shuffles across the carpet and flings her arms round her mum's legs.

'You are not a bad mum. You're a good one and you try really hard. It wasn't your fault.'

'No, it was yours, Sheena.' The other sister turns round too and flicks off the telly.

'You pushed Ali.'

'I didn't', Jai.'

'You did!'

'He rolled.'

'I thought he was too fat to fall through that window!'

'I bounced.'

This is the first time Ali had spoken, a husky, cusp-of-puberty voice. He grins coyly from the couch and suddenly we are all laughing.

Ali looks delightedly at us.

'You are a fucking idiot, Ali.'

'Jai! All of you are idiots, no "fucking word" in this house, Jai, and I am fed up of you all,' says poor Mrs Oppah, whose shoulders are shaking.

51

'Still, no harm done, nurse, eh?' says Sheena hopefully. 'I mean Ali, yeah, but he'll mend.'

'He could have been killed. He's a walking miracle, the doctors say.'

'Rolling.'

We laugh some more.

'You're called Sylvie, the school nurse. I know you from Fat Club,' says Ali.

'Fat Club didn't' work for you, though did it? What about the poor man Ali fell on?' says Jai.

'Yeah, you should of seen the other guy, Sylvie,' chuckles Ali.

'Not funny!' but we are all still laughing.

Ali, Mrs Oppah and I settle down to make a care plan, so that his little school, which is just around the corner from their building, can support him appropriately, in his phased return. The four flights of stairs to their flat are an obstacle, as the lift is often out of order, but the four weeks while Ali's leg is in a cast will pass quickly, I reassure Mrs Oppah, with more confidence than I feel. Ali seems unperturbed about remaining indefinitely on his ottoman.

'And we can arrange for the girls to bring work up from school – are you both still at Piccadilly Primary?' I ask

'Nah. I'm at Langham Girls. Don't you remember me? I came and ate my lunch in your drop in one time, Sylvie, with my friends, before running club.'

'I thought you looked familiar....', a lie she will detect, but I have a problem remembering faces – terrible trait in a school nurse. I'd like to say I remember other things, but maybe this is fancy. They care when

52

we don't keep them in mind, of course they do. I keep them in mind, all of them, but can't remember their faces very well.

'I wish we could of helped the man.'

'What do you mean, Jai?'

'The man what Ali fell on. When we all ran down to see what had happened and Ali had fallen through the restaurant awning, he landed on this man…'.

'Yeah, a man who was eating at the Italian. His dinner was splatted everywhere and it was funny.'

'Shut the fuck up, Sheena.'

'It was though! It did have its funny side. You were laughing a minute ago…'.

'Sheena, shut up! But Sylvie, the man was okay in the end, so it's not like he died or anything, but when he was lying on the pavement, I wasn't sure and I wanted to help him and Ali and…'

'Jai?'

'And I didn't know how, you know?' Jai had tears welling now and brushed them roughly away with her sleeve.

'If only I had some first aid or something, some training yeah? I wouldn't feel so fucking useless standing there. There was poor Ali, all broken, stupid moron, then the man, with his head all bleeding, lying on the floor… and no one doing nothing, except wailing and screaming!'

'It must have been very upsetting,' I say, looking round at the family, who all nod solemnly, not laughing now.

'What did you do, Jai?'

'I called the ambulance on my smartphone, didn't I? All I could think to do. So stupid.'

'Listen to me Jai, that wasn't stupid, not at all. In an emergency the first rule is to check for danger and if you're not sure, then it's entirely appropriate to call for help. You did the right thing. You acted appropriately.'

'That's what I told her,' said Mrs Oppah. 'Listen to the nurse.'

Jai shakes her head, shuffling on the carpet, but her eyes meet mine.

'Is there a class I could do? You know, to learn more – like what we are meant to do if it happens again?'

'I'm not planning on falling out of any more windows!' quips the little emperor.

'Fuck off, Ali. You know what I mean, Sylvie? First Aid. They do it in Year Nine, but I'm only in Year Eight. Could you guys run it, at the Centre?'

We wrap up our little care plan, with Mrs Oppah apologising for Jai's language and her own maternal shortcomings and all of the Oppahs shouting, laughing and swearing at each other and I leave shortly after, marveling that Ali didn't suffer any head injury or worse, wondering about the First Aid seed that clever, cross Jai has planted.

Down below, in the courtyard of the Buildings, the girl with the plaits sits on the step like it's 1950.

'It's getting cold, Kayleigh, aren't you going in?' I ask.

Kayleigh chews on a plait and shrugs.

'Yeah, maybe. Them okay up there?'

She gestures up to the Oppah's flat. 'Noisy bunch, aren't they, nurse?'

54

'Did you see the accident happen, Kayleigh?'

'Well, not happen, because it was out on the street and my mum doesn't let me out there when she's working, but we all rushed round. Couldn't tell what was blood and what was ketchup.'

'Would you come to a First Aid class if I ran one?'

'Where?'

'In the Square, say.'

'Might do, yeah.'

'Would your brother?'

'He ain't my brother. Might do. I want to be a doctor when I grow up.'

'Ever thought of nursing?'

'Nope.'

No, no one does these days, but whose fault is that?

'Let me know if you start up a class, Miss... yeah?'

'I will. Take care now, Kayleigh,' I add uselessly. Kayleigh has been taking care of herself for years, I get the feeling.

'Is your mum working now?'

'Yep.'

Seriously Sylvie! Are there many working girls with kids still in Soho, Sylvie?

I think there are prostitutes in every town, aren't there, Finn?

Cromer, even?

Maybe 'downtown Cromer', not the posh part where you live.

55

Finn chuckles: Everything is blamed on downtown Cromer: crime, sex, drugs and iniquity. As though the ones who dwell in the respectable upper echelons shine like the lighthouse.

I expect there are Kayleighs in Cromer, though. If a child is bright and canny, like Kayleigh, she will look out for herself pretty well and cover for her mother. And to be fair, it wasn't a working girl's child who fell out of a window, it was Ali, whose mum is there all the time and couldn't be more attentive.

Finn says: And I've been wondering, are there any school nurses left in Norfolk, Sylvie?

And the answer to this one hangs in the air.

Chapter Five

I shut the door on a houseful of sleeping teens as I set off for work this morning. There is an inset day at their school, for which they read 'lie-in'. The spring sun is bright on the old Abbey walls, new leaves appear again, surprising me. Teenage children miss this time of the morning if they possibly can. Mine are unimpressed by my extolling the joys of spring in the air.

What's the great surprise? Spring happens every year, Mum.'

Maybe it means more as we get older.

Maybe. I just wish the birds would shut up.

During term time we also live in a school, by virtue of my partner's job; an old and famous independent school where some of the world's most ostensibly privileged are educated. I might have high ideals about fairness and equality but because some people choose to send their children to this particular school, we are lucky to live here, which gives us insight into another school world, of course.

And next door there is the choir school, a 'Royal Peculiar', where thirty extraordinary children serve Church and Queen by singing the services every day. They are miniature awe-inspiring professional musicians and when they are not singing or studying they are playing football outside our window. So, more school worlds still.

The choristers are up and awake, on the other side of the green. Thirty boys between eight and twelve line up in their black cloaks, like quiet, orderly crows.

Their silence is purposeful, not oppressed. As soon as they have crossed the Yard, into the Song School they will burst into song, under the direction of their choirmaster. These are boys who love to sing, so no hardship in their disciplined early start. Being a chorister is not a life that works for every child. Sometimes even the very musical, very keen ones become a little overwhelmed.

The boys are not meant to stop and talk when they're walking over to choir practice, but this morning, as most mornings, a few of the older ones smile and we acknowledge each other, as neighbors.

Old fashioned souls, wise heads on tiny shoulders. young musicians, exposed to the most profound choral sounds, working with some of England's finest musicians, touring the world… Is this good for them? Is it better than bumbling through a more natural primary school life in one of the schoolyards nearby? This is hard to judge. Their lives are so definitely different and two Children's Acts of 1989 and 2004, as well as caring and dedicated staff, make boarding a potentially positive experience nowadays. Because I love the church music these children make, my respect and gratitude for them is infinite, my glasses possibly rose-tinted.

Sometimes the sound of their ordinary assembly hymn carries on a morning breeze across the yard, as I step out. And every time I am blown away by this sound; thirty incredible trebles singing their morning hymn, naturally and lustily. I prefer this to their more formal singing in the abbey, where they execute such complex pieces, different music each day. That is the world famous choir on show, this, a more intimate time, an everyday start to their extraordinary day, and they sing like the birds in the trees.

Theirs is a cloistered life, literally, in a space which lends itself to hundreds of years of peace, contemplation and learning, until the boys swarm out mid-morning, to scream and let off steam, playing football on the green.

This morning I cross Victoria Street and head over St James's Park, then up the Duke of York Steps and into Piccadilly. A different world so swiftly. There are so many adjacent worlds.

Oddly, there is a goose in a tree, next to the lake. I acknowledge the goose, who looks surprised to have arrived there. I make a mental note to mention the goose in the tree to Ricci or someone, because these are the tiny absurd details of an ordinary day that can slip past unmarked.

The flowerbeds are newly vibrant, for something official to do with the Queen, and I am wrong footed, as almost every morning, by temporary barriers erected to contain soldiers and a marching band, practicing their parade.

At the bottom of Shaftesbury Avenue nestles one of our schools, Piccadilly Primary. The old Victorian brick hall is painted bright pink, the classrooms daffodil yellow, pea-green, tugboat blue. Opposite this school is a lap-dancing club and we are properly into Soho, no masking that, but inside the school smells of crayons and playdough, plimsols and Copydex; primary school world. It's an hour too early for school, but I pop in to drop off a letter for a parent, whom I'm hoping to meet later in the week.

The head teacher, Mr Simpson, is chatting to the office manager when I arrive.

'Sylvie, just the person. Can we get in early with Year Six Sex and Relationships this term?'

'Hello, Will. Before their SATS exams do you mean? I'm doing All Saints' SRE talk this week, actually. Although they have stipulated we call it RSE – relationships before sex, which seems sensible enough.'

'Um, no, after SATS I think, so later in the term, three sessions, but I know how booked up you guys get. Have you heard that some parents are boycotting SATS this year? I can't say I blame them. The questions are so hard now I can hardly do them myself. Is it just you and Alan for the twenty schools, still?'

'Yes, though we are working on recruiting…' I tail off, as I see his polite eyes glazing over at this familiar sentence and cannot blame him, because I bore myself with our worn out narrative. We school nurses are growing tired of defending our dying service….

'Oh well, good luck with all that, Sylvie. Straightened times. Must go. Oh, did you hear about Ali Oppah? The kids are calling him Space—'

'Hopper, yes. I heard. His poor mum.'

'Quite. But it is funny, because he's . . . no, that would be mean. Mean and wrong, of course. Fat isn't a word we use these days and quite right too. Could you do an anaphylaxis refresher, too? We have three more kids starting with severe allergy. Is everyone allergic to something nowadays?'

'Even the air that we breathe is toxic. I'll talk to Alan today. One of us can do the training, I'm sure.'

'Thanks Sylvie. That's great. Must dash though.'

In some areas of the country, I hear they are adopting systematic, organised models of school nursing, based on a sound public health profiling of each school population. Good for them. A few years back, when it looked as though school nursing was going to be invested in, there might have been someone in our large public health department to ask about adopting this degree of professionalism. But with numbers and resources as they are, 'the search for health needs', a pre-requisite of the public health nurse, consists of Alan and me scrabbling about optimistically trying to meet the needs where they arise.

'Will, can I ask what would you think to my setting up a First Aid course for the children? Something Jai Oppah said…'

'Jai? Oh, I liked her. Furious little person, the opposite of her brother 'so-laid-back-he-fell–out-of a-window' Ali, but good head on her shoulders. How's she doing at Langham Girls?'

'She's doing well, I think. But in theory you'd be okay with a first aid course, if we found somewhere nearby to run it? We would cover anaphylaxis and asthma.'

'Of course. Really good plan. Not here though, I'm afraid. Completely booked out to the Chinese Adult Education after school. Bye'

It's still only eight a.m. I step round a road cleaner on the tiny pavement and continue to the clinic.

Clearing rubbish for the day is a big morning thing in Soho. Cleansing the streets of debris from the night before, each and every day. Rubbish includes humans now. In my average walk to work I may now count twenty persons lying in dusty doorways. Sometimes I leave a coffee or a bun by a barely moving sleeping bag, often I don't. Never now do I stop to properly check if the person is actually breathing. What sort of world, when we are inert to the concept of half-conscious people lying in the road? When my children were small, we might pass a stray cat on the way to school, but never a stray person.

These things are done when the wood is green.

Exactly, Theo.

The Gospel of Luke.

I remember.

The Westminster Council electronic cleaning vans have an unintentionally spiteful method of spraying freezing, foamy water jets up the curb to dislodge old gum, soaking the flimsy bedding of the hapless homeless. What do the kids make of this on their way in? And of the tired neon signs announcing SEX with the morning baking smells, as they file into the sanctuary of their school for a new day?

I slip along Old Compton Street, past Berwick, (where Ali descended from his Building), then Wardour, then Dean, then Frith, stopping to pick up a little takeaway coffee at the bottom of Frith Street. Soho has spoilt me with cafe life; it used to be that I would roll into whichever clinic was my base, stick the communal kettle on, rummage around for someone's teabag or coffee granule, occasionally buy my own jar and hope the milk had not gone off. Nowadays, I'm drawn into the lovely cafes, the infinite promise of each uniquely roasted bean. Often I buy a bun too. Fivers slip away as easily as the souls of curb-dwellers past. My favourite coffee bar bakes cinnamon buns on Fridays, so has become a natural resting place for Alan and me to have a weekly look through his student portfolio, giving Alan an entirely rose-tinted example of the average school nursing day, I expect.

Today I stop at Nero's, convincing myself that I need a proper, hot coffee.

Wake up and smell the coffee, Sylvie.

Not Luke's gospel, that, Theo.

No, but something Luke might have said had he been a doctor in Soho, rather than Palestine in 75 AD?

City life is this way. Glimpses of heaven in the hell. Sightings of hell on the golden pavements.

I reach the Square, with its quaint mock-Tudor house, the campanile tower of St James' Catholic church behind and our own old hospital building to the right. Engraved above the elegant high ward windows;

SUPPORTED BY VOLUNTARY CONTRIBUTIONS

Sadly, no longer. Recently our NHS Trust sold this building and we now rent it back, square metre by extortionate square metre, which is why Ricci, the team and I reside in the basement.

Through the smooth oak door with my plastic pass, into the marble hall.

Morning Sally, Morning Glory.

And I'm sure I hear Glory's wheezy Irish chuckle on the air, before Ricci hurtles in behind me.

'Hello Sylvie, oh my God, I went out to Brent yesterday, for mandatory training – it's a barren wilderness there. No shops, not even a Nero! How do these people live? Ah, how lucky we are! Lovely, lovely Soho.'

'Lovely Soho,' I agree

'Amazing old hall this, isn't it? Art Deco.'

'Arts and Crafts, I heard.'

'Oh yes. Art something, definitely. You got time for a coffee, Sylvie? It's still early.'

I consider for a second only. I've already bought that one coffee, tasks on our bossy computer system await me and I need to prepare a lecture for the students tomorrow.

'Little quick one? Tinsy winsy Macchiato? I have Nelly outside, who's longing to catch up and there is something we need to discuss. Something serious.'

His face is suddenly not smiley, his eyes solemn.

'Go on then, five minutes.'

Nelly sits alert and present, tied to the railing. She leaps up, wagging her curly tail as Ricci and I come over.

'She really is the most beautiful dog, Ricci. So intelligent in the face.'

'Of course, she takes after me.'

Ricci unties Nelly, rubbing her nose affectionately. 'I have Theo to thank – if I hadn't gone to talk to him, I would never have given birth to Nelly the dog. She has given my life a new purpose. Soho Joes? They let Nelly sit outside and it's a nice morning.'

'Perfect. My turn to buy.'

We sit outside on the wooden pews provided. Each person who passes has a little pat for Nelly. She absorbs their random love patiently, accepts it as her due.

Ricci sips his tinsy macchiato, focusing on me with his sudden attention, quick delivery.

'So, it's like this Sylvie; you know I was encouraging last week, when you came back? Trying to be optimistic, putting a brave face on community nursing.'

'Yes. You enthused me.'

'Hmm. Well, I've changed my mind. It's all up. Health visiting and school nursing are going to the dogs – sorry Nelly, offensive expression. I have seen the budget for our services and the local authority forecast for the next year and it really isn't pretty. Sylvie, you and I have been sleep walking, with our old fashioned aspirations and our Nightingale values. The Chancellor of England doesn't share our vision, for God's sake, did you see the budget? The Health Secretary has managed to alienate even the junior doctors, so heaven help us. And the country's money pot is empty anyway. Even if it weren't there are precious few people who get public health. Upstream thinking, my arse. We are drowning, Sylvie. We are doomed! And the pressure is beginning to show in all the health visitors too, despite the nominal investments of the past few years. After the wave of lovely 'old school' practitioners who are retiring this year, we will still have fewer health visit before the 'Call to Action'.

'Funny phrase that for a recruitment movement, wasn't it? War-like.'

'Appropriately so, as it turns out. I have vacant caseloads appearing like holes in a Swiss cheese, like gaps in an Alzheimer brain. We are miles behind on our New Birth Visits – they'll be toddlers by the time we reach them, we may need Nelly to cover clinics at this rate and that's before dear Molly and Grace leave.'

'Are they leaving?'

Molly and Grace are two elderly Caribbean health visitors, very much of the old school, who have worked this patch since the nineteen seventies. They remember when hippies littered the Soho Square lawn, making daisy chains and smoking pot. When 'battered wives' were newly spoken of, though old in concept, when flares were 'in' for the first time. They live next door to each other in the Buildings near Berwick Street, two floors below Ali Oppah. Old time Soho dwellers, theatre and exhibition goers, compulsive followers of Time Out in their time off, always have time for their mothers and families.

'They've had enough, Sylvie. This latest NHS re-structuring, along with our own ill-advised shift to yet another crappy computer system, has done for them. Have you seen the latest generic message you get every time you switch it on? 'You have twenty-nine thousand tasks awaiting. This impacts detrimentally on your organisation, blah blah, blah…'.It's not our Trust's fault as such, but It's Orwellian! So you are down to one beautiful, impossibly talented student, Alan. And I have one man - me, Molly and Grace – well Moll really, Grace is pretty deranged most days - just until they pack up for good – and a dog, Nelly.'

'Nelly improves maternal mood.'

'She does, she does. Forget the Woolley Questions and Listening Visits for the post- natally depressed, all they really need is Nelly. But she and

I can't get round every new birth, from Paddington Green to Pimlico.'

'Have you talked to the 'Powers That Be'?'

'I've tried, but you know how it is. There's no malice in the individuals, none, but the Trust is expanding as fast as possible, claiming more and services outside Central London, so that we keep us as a viable competitive entity. Here in the centre, we are expensive and with the rent-capping policy, the demographic is shifting. Our families are being moved out to far flung boroughs, your school populations are diminishing rapidly. Soho is being hollowed out.'

'You see it in the building projects, literally, don't you?' I say.

'Looking up at what was a block of old fashioned flats, to see only a façade, blue sky through empty windows and a structure all held up with steel girders, ready for re-development. 'I'm not leaving Soho, Soho is leaving me' I read in The Week.'

'Exactly, So the property developers can build their luxury accommodation for multi-nationals who will never live here. Behind the facade it's as fragile as a stage set.' No community, this. Time to go. Maybe our work is done…'.

Leave not a rack behind.

'Oh Nelly,'… I stroke her soft wet nose. 'Your master is sad today.'

'I am elegiac, Sylvie. This feels like…'.

He moves his arms expansively. Up the road a young man crouched, huddled in a grey blanket begins to play a recorder, two notes only; 'A', 'B', 'A', 'B'.

Ricci groans '… Oh God, not him again. He won't get much money playing that. He's a crack addict anyway. Breaks my heart, but you see – he is a metaphor for how it all really is, Sylvie. He is sitting on the sunny side of the street, playing two notes on his fucking recorder, to keep his pathetic little skeleton clothed and his habit alive, while the world ends, not with a bang but a whimper.'

'Ricci!'

'I know! Hark at me. But it's how I feel, you know? We have tried so hard, but…'.

'Come with me this afternoon to teach sex at All Saints? That will cheer you up.'

'Oh go on, then.' Ricci springs up, grinning, without a moment's hesitation. It is easy to sway his mood temporarily.

'Nelly, it's only a diversion Sylvie's offering us, but it's a good one, isn't it? The world may be ending, but children still need to learn about periods, don't they?'

'Certainly they do.' I say. 'Chad Varah founded The Samaritans on that very premise.'

'Is that right?'

'A young girl in his parish committed suicide because she had started her period and thought she was suffering an incurable illness. He vowed that no one should die of such pitiful ignorance.'

'So wise. He was a vicar in the City, wasn't he?'

'Yes. St Stephen Walbrook. And Ricci – I've had an idea to run some First Aid on the Square. Will you help?'

'Brilliant.'

Ricci is easily diverted, if not cheered.

Walking back around our corner, we let ourselves back into our marble hall of dreams. Glory's ghost welcomes us invisibly, Sally smiles benignly from beyond the veil.

***

'So we've established some ground rules; no question is a silly question, don't ask personal questions of each other and do respect what everyone has to say. And today it's absolutely fine to giggle, because all this is funny, as well as private and important, isn't it, Ricci?'

'Absolutely.'

'So let's start by thinking about the changes that are happening to everyone, just now. What are some of those changes? Hands up'

'Hands up' is an old fashioned, redundant teaching method, I suspect, but the children and their lovely form teacher forgive us because we are visitors, not teachers. Redundant mainly, because of course their hands are up. All thirty have a hand reaching to touch the ceiling, their little shirts coming adrift from their trousers, showing ribs on some, podgy muffin top and lack of ribs on many. Where does this blissful enthusiasm go, when the darling Year Sixes move on through the puberty we are going to be exploring in this lesson? I love Year Six.

Ricci is less sure, having usually worked with older teens and young adults, but he is my walking talking evidence-base on sexual health, for the more challenging questions. Heaven to have him alongside this afternoon. And Nelly too, lying obediently on a bean bag in The Quiet Corner, one eye open to their antics. I'll allude to her when I explain that all mammals reproduce in the same way, if it doesn't offend her dignity. She hasn't had puppies yet.

All Saints, a broad minded, broad church primary school, gives us a pretty free rein when we come to talk puberty. Our Catholic schools can be more exacting; demanding that, after I have inexpertly drawn a lopsided uterus on the white board, with a spongey womb wall either side and fallopian tubes for a microscopic egg to travel down, we stop right there. Periods, but no fertilising of the egg. And if or rather when, the bright question comes, as it invariably does,

'How is the egg fertilised?' we are instructed to move on swiftly, not lying, but not elucidating either;

'That is something you will learn all about it in biology, at secondary school.'

Ricci struggles with this tailored approach to the facts of life, believing that in sexual health education, no holes should be barred. I agree completely, but along with many school nurses have learnt that it's better to be there in some capacity, with the opportunity to explain the role of the school nurse as someone they can come and talk to in confidence in their secondary schools too, than excluded from their education completely, for the sake of a few emotive sentences.

But those sentences you miss out are the reason we are all here at all.

Okay, ridiculous, I know. And cowardly, even. I should just be brave and say it how it is.

'We are starting new schools, Miss'

'You are! Where are you all going?'

They offer up all their destinations excitedly, having heard shortly before the Easter holidays, in the post.

'Langham Girls, Miss.'

'You can call me Sylvie, not Miss. We are Sylvie and Ricci, and Nelly.' Nelly pricks up an ear at her name. They laugh.

'Nurses are usually called by their first names, partly because we end up talking about things that teachers don't usually mention every day,

69

although you can always talk to your teacher if you want to, can't they Miss Bullen? Langham Girls - great. How many are going there?'

Half the girls put up their hands.

'And I'm the school nurse there, too, so you'll be used to seeing me around. Others?'

'Victoria Boys, Miss, I mean Sylvie.'

'Lovely. How many? My colleague Alan is the school nurse there. He is coming in next week, to go through any questions you may have from today. Any others?'

There are lots of different schools, some in borough, some out and some venturing off to board at one of the old charity schools founded for the deserving poor of Tudor London and now housed in spacious countryside, ringed with woods and downlands fair.

'I wouldn't call Victoria Boys lovely, Sylvie. My brother goes there and he says it's a shit hole.'

'Ashley!' warns Miss Bullen.

'Well, it's hardly Hogwarts, Miss. And Sylvie said we could use rude words today.'

'Not in general conversation, Ashley. Only pertaining to parts of the body.'

'Well a shit-hole is a part of the…'.

'That's enough, Ashley.' says Miss Bullen firmly, making me a bit nervous.

Ricci is rapt.

We chat on about general change for a while, then work our way round to the specific body changes, these smooth, shining babes can begin to expect in the next few months. One taller boy child, who already has a partial moustache starts us off;

'Hairs grow, Sylvie.'

'They do, they do, well done. How about you take your big pieces of paper, draw a body like a gingerbread person and then begin to fill in all the changes. Hairs, where they grow on the boys and the girls and some of the other changes too, if you can think of them.'

Of course they can think of them. They set about this task, with Miss Bullen patiently presiding and Ricci leaping from table to table, helping with the detail. Then we talk through the changes in a properly no holes barred fashion, of which we can be proud, encouraging questions;

'I get confused about how many holes a girl has, Sylvie and Ricci.'

'I sympathise' says Ricci.

'It can be incredibly confusing. Can we draw this on the board, Miss Bullen?'

'By all means, Ricci.'

'So – here is the one that everybody has and this one is called….'.

'A bum hole.' They chorus.

'Well done. And what comes out of a bum, or shall we call it a bottom hole?'

'Poo!'

'Excellent. We can cover the Latin names later. Well, then there are the other two holes that a girl has and these are called...'.

And on we go, Dr Ricci Jones and I, until the facts of life are fully explained, to the incredulity of some, though most knew already. We round off our afternoon with all of them gathering round Nelly in The Quiet Corner for Miss Bullen to read the old but splendidly un-dated

Mummy Laid an Egg', by Babette Cole, an excellent story in which embarrassed parents are too inept to explain the facts of life and their sensible children save the day. You're never too grown up for a story.

'So now you all know what's what, you can go home and tell your parents and other people who look after you, what we have talked about today. They may find it awkward, but persevere with them and be kind. It's important. Fill up your question box with your queries and we will answer them all next week, when we come back with Alan. You don't have to put your names on the questions if you are a bit shy…'.

To bring them back down to earth, I canvas them about the First Aid Course.

'We plan to start next Wednesday after school – 3.45pm in Soho Square. If it's raining, we will repair to the clinic. What do you think?'

There is much enthusiasm about this, too and Miss Bullen agrees to put something in the Friday newsletter. Harnessing Year Six energy might yet be the way to run the world.

'That was the best afternoon we've spent in ages, wasn't it Nelly?. Is school nursing always that much fun? I can't wait for next week's questions and I totally can't wait for First Aid.'

Chapter Six

By the end of the week we have twenty potential first aiders ready for the course it seems Ricci and I are going to be running, for children of all ages. Venue Soho Square if fine, the hallway of our centre if wet.

'As if we haven't got enough to do, with the sixteen primaries and four secondary schools to cover, but Jai's was such a good idea, don't you think, Ricci? I couldn't resist.'

'Alfresco First Aid... divine!' gushes Ricci, then with a doubtful glance and ruffle of his beard; 'Are you remotely qualified, Sylvie? I mean we all know a bit as nurses, don't we, but I'm not sure I would know how to explain it to others like we did the sex ed... and even though The Powers leave us pretty much alone these days, I'm sure there is a policy we should be following...'.

'I am as it happens, qualified I mean. And I have a dual heritage extended family of manikins, including seven Baby Annie manikins.'

In order to swell our family coffers, I have been teaching paediatric and adult emergency first aid for several years, every Saturday. It has been useful, even essential for financial reasons. This would be different; teaching the likes of Jai and the exuberant primary school kids at their own pace, linking to our local schools, contributing to the extra-curricular, potentially a refreshing change, I've been thinking.'

'Oh, phew, that's okay then. Though Sylvie, have you noticed how quiet The Powers have gone of late? It's almost as though they've forgotten us.'

'We're in the eye of the storm. It's quite a maelstrom of tenders and bids raging out there, especially in the Outer Boroughs, I've heard.'

Ricci pulls a face at the horror of dwelling in the Outer Boroughs.

'Poor them. We'd be shit at those senior jobs, Ricci. Meanwhile, perfect if they leave us be for a bit. I've been impressed by the enthusiasm for the First Aid idea, from teachers and from the children. And there's a sound evidence base, in that we have high admissions to A & E for silly reasons, so we might even see those diminish.'

'Evaluate and write it up! Perfect public health. I'll bring some tooth rotting biscuits and orange squash, so it doesn't get too worthy. And I'll bring Nelly. Do you do doggy CPR? When do we start?'

'Wednesday after school. I've got the University SCPHN students tomorrow.'

'Ah, those darlings. I'm going in to start their Nurse Prescribing next week. I hear Daphne and Chloe are having kittens with this year's set.'

'They are not all model students, the likes of Alan, apparently.'

'Alan is adorable. A scraping the barrel bunch, otherwise, I heard. Can any of them even write a sentence and add up?'

'Well, I still can't add up…'.

'No, but you passed your drug tests back in the day, on the wards, didn't you? Remember '100% or you've killed a patient'. They used to be refreshingly blunt in our day.'

'That was the only maths exam I ever got 100% for, so I suppose it worked.'

'Ah, the good old days when 'reflective practice' meant; 'have a good cry in the sluice, dry your eyes on your pinny and move on.'

'I'm liking the vision of you in a pinny, Ricci. Anyway, I'm at the Uni tomorrow, so we'll see. I suspect Daphne and Chloe exaggerate and they are as clever as ever. Fancy another coffee and bun?'

'Yes, yes! Do you call everything a bun, Sylvie? I'm after a decent Victoria sponge or Bakewell slice, me.'

***

'They've all been so naughty – disrespectful, eating in the lectures, late, everything. I've read them the riot act this morning, I'm afraid, Sylvie. It's got quite ridiculous'

This is Daphne's summer semester rant every year. She is not talking about teenagers, but the qualified, adult nurse students who are undertaking the aforementioned SCPHN course. Daphne has run the course for years and as students we all disappoint her collectively, every year without fail.

'I am this far… *this far*… from complete despair about them!' she will rail cheerfully, squeezing thumb and finger together, squinting jewel-like green eyes merrily at me.

'The worst set ever. Nothing will come of them. I mean would you have faith in their health visiting competence if they came round to visit you when you had three children under five? No! You would take one look at them, sit them down and make *them* a cup of tea, wouldn't you? Hopeless. I despair. Never has there been such a year.'

'Daphne, they can't be as bad as we were, when you taught my set. And we've turned out okay. There may be something about being herded together again in a student capacity that makes us regress…'.

'Argh! Sylvie, you were angels in comparison. You had intelligence, intellect and failing that, native wit. Your class could write an essay, string a sentence together. This year – we even have one who insists on breast feeding in the class and look at that one in the mauve knitted bobble hat, I ask you? Would you visit a newly delivered mother in a *bobble hat?*'

The students are filing in now, looking soulful and subdued.

'I truly can't bear the sight of them any longer, Sylvie. Chloe feels just the same. Can I leave you to it? You know how to start up the overhead and all that, don't you?'

'I'll be fine, Sylvie. Go. A coffee together after, maybe?'

'I won't have time. I won't have a moment. Would that I had! It's not a breeze here, like your gentle community days, you know. These wretched students sap my life blood. Bye now and thanks again.'

Daphne gives me a kiss on the cheek and whizzes away, diminutive, immaculate, a nattily dressed embodiment of chic, complete with twinset, pearls and tidy shoes.

'Love to Chloe, too.'

She smiles – how does she keep her lipstick on so perfectly, all day? Ana would be all respect.'

'Will do.'

Chloe, fellow professor, is of course the antithesis of tiny, frenetic Daphne. Tall, calm laconic and French, her easy going demeanor gently masks a huge brain. They have run this course together for fifteen years, guiding hundreds of nurses through the academic rigours of this applied public health degree, into school nursing or health-visitor-dom. Recently, as research into the importance of a good start in life and Early Years became incontrovertible, the government has begun to reappraise the role of the health visitor. Historically, health visitors had been those extra bright or extra middle class nurses who were far sighted enough to realise that being a graduate would enhance everything. The last of this rare breed were coming to retirement age now and at the eleventh hour the government launched a 'Call to Action' recruitment drive, with – astonishing for the current times – significant financial investment attached. The impact for the likes of Daphne and Chloe was to double their workload, as SCPHN student numbers swelled, to fill the shortfall. Was there money for school nursing, too? After all, the years from baby to five are important, but five to nineteen year olds matter too, don't they? The parents of the future? The short answer from on high: no.

'But school nurses have always been resourceful. What better time to jump on the band wagon and demonstrate your worth?', extolled our inspirational chief nursing directorate.

That is what we have tried to do and that is why I am here, enrolled as an extra lecturer, with links to practice, to help cover gaps.

They've all shuffled in now, distinctly subdued from Daphne's dressing down. I beam out at them.

'Hello, you lot in trouble?'

They laugh. There is, after all, an adolescent in all of us. Easy for me, they are putty in my hands, because as is so often the case, in schools or other settings, school nurse can be 'good cop'. We can deliver a slightly more light-hearted lesson, then slip away. And my opening gambit for teaching them about the assessment models we use in practice every day may not be so hard for them. I bring up my first slide: *Still Small Voice.*

I have been bold enough to reference my own model and they are going to learn about it today, to add to their 'bag' of assessment tools and maybe pull out one morning, in their own schools: 'Now, if you can cast your minds back, I'd like you to all imagine yourselves at fifteen…'.

The students become absorbed in their own genograms, wandering back through their own family histories, pondering their own lives in the context of the common assessment framework, a useful addition to the assessment toolbox, devised back in the Millennium year, but still so useful today:

Assessment Framework

Then we weave into our consideration the two key concepts of attachment and containment. They have already learnt about attachment theory; it has been staple to their year. Despite Daphne's gloomy account, they seem every bit as bright and interested as past years, of course they are. One student school nurse is perfectly happy to rattle off to me what attachment theory is, in summary: 'The early relationship with a significant caregiver which provides the blueprint for all future relationships'

'Good. Can you say a little more about what Bowlby meant by that?'

'Babies are biologically programmed to seek the physical and emotional proximity of a significant caregiver who will ensure their survival, protect them from harm and provide a secure base from which to explore the world. If the significant caregiver is able to respond in a predictable and sensitive way to the infant's behavioural cues, the infant develops an internal working model of him/herself as being able to activate a response from others, as being a valuable and worthy individual capable of inspiring a loving response from others - and the infant also gains a sense that others can be relied on in times of need.'

'God! I mean Good! Good knowledge! Um, have you memorised that, what's your name?'

'Sonny, Yes. It seemed important, well vital really.'

The others nod, approvingly and I'm aware of a conscious struggle not to give in to clichéd observation about Chinese students working harder and having better memories than most of us. Have the rest of us lost the capacity to learn things by rote?

Is she even Chinese, Mum? Check your unconscious racism, there? You're terrible.

'Yes, quite. Wonderful. And if you like attachment theory, you're going to love containment. Bion's theory of Containment,1959 was a revelation to me, when I first learned about it. Anyone want to have a go at explaining this concept, key to health visiting and school nursing practice? Have any of you heard about it before, perhaps?'

Most faces look a bit blank at this one, but Sonny pipes up:

'The idea with containment is that the parent is able to help the child to process intense feels of emotion or anxiety, rather than feeling overwhelmed by them. This helps the child to learn to understand and manage his/her own feelings. When children are not overwhelmed by feelings they have a greater capacity to make sense of and enjoy their surroundings'.

'Exactly. Thank you Sonny. Does that make sense to you all?'

I'm stunned by lovely Sonny. I read them all Donald Winnicott's passage describing how a natural mother will try to comfort a crying child in lots of ways, not becoming overwhelmed themselves, but letting the child grumble on in their own time, providing a safe vessel for the child's mixed emotions.

Sonny volunteers: "Is the idea that in some ways health visitors and school nurses are able to help parents manage their overwhelming feelings, so that they can think calmly and creatively for themselves about any difficulties that they are experiencing?'

I agree that, yes, this would be an ideal worth aiming for and Sonny gets us thinking to what extent we can do this. We also consider containment in relation to our own experience, linking back to the genograms. Cycling home, I know that this kind of teaching is every bit as interesting as Sex Ed to Year Sixes. Lucky job, to be able to do both and other things, stuck with no group for any length of time. Like partying without the washing up. Poor Miss Bowen, Daphne and Chloe, have to do everything in-between with their learners. How lucky am I?

As I wheel my bike up to our front door, my sixteen-year-old daughter is smoking on the doorstep.

'I wish you wouldn't…', I start, unnecessarily

She casts me a reproachful look, red-eyed, blotchy faced.

'It's over. We've split up.'

'Oh darling.' I get down on the doorstep, to hug her smokey body, pat her springy hair.

'It's the end of the world, mum.'

And while it is not the end of the world it is to her, of course. And when it comes to holding, being alongside, containment in action, I feel as completely ineffectual as every mum in the history of the world, ever.

Chapter Seven

When the afternoon of our first first aid class arrives, preparation is not extensive. We are in late April now and the afternoon is serendipitous; sunny and warm, with a kind breeze, so we can lay out rugs picnic-style, on the east side of the square in a hopeful spirit. I squeeze in a quick text exchange with Finn:

Ha! Lucky you. Come to Cromer, two coats Cromer'... still freezing here, Sylvie.

The lazy north-easterly goes through you, not round you?

That's the one. Sunny, but freezing, with the spirit of the town planners as bitter and unrelenting as the wind.

No movement on your plans, then?

Not really – we have all the goodwill and a sound business plan, we have pledges of daily baking from hundreds of Cromer residents, but still a way to go with the officials' demands. I think we will get there, then I damn myself for naive optimism and struggle to remember why we are even bothering, what compels us. You know how it is...

As I set out my hideous, but strangely compelling resuscitation family, in their matching tee-shirts and baby-gros (sandcastles and 'Come to Cromer' logos), I think about Finn battling it out on the bracing Cromer coast. It is always hard to imagine others' lives. Cromer seems remote from Soho Square.

'Do you think anyone will come, Alan?

Alan surveys the square, then points to a little procession of people heading our way

'Well here's a start.'

'Hiya Sylvie. Give us a hand with this chair, he's fucking heavy?'

Up the picturesque city garden path comes Jai Oppah, concentrating hard to manoeuvre Ali, who sits resplendent in a large red wheelchair, his left leg sticking out, still encased thigh to toe in its now grubby white cast.

'And the fucking lift was broken, so we bumped him down the stairs.'

Ali is beaming his wide, Buddha smile.

'I'm well cushioned.' He is an incredibly amiable boy.

Behind them trails Sheena, looking less enthusiastic and Kayleigh, still chewing a bedraggled plait.

The boy whose name I don't yet know, but remember from the buildings, is kicking a ball along behind the girls.

'What's your friend's name, Kayleigh?'

'Him, oh he ain't my friend no more. And he won't stay, I bet ya.'

'Oh and look!' says Alan, turning.

Four more year six pupils we know from the All Saints' sex education class are approaching from the other side of the park

I move to welcome them all enthusiastically, finding myself extraordinarily moved that they have bothered to come at all, even though the class was of course Jai's idea.

'I'd rather been hoping Plank would come,' said Alan quietly.

'With Angus, Sidney and Lloyd, you know? I did a home visit to encourage them and Cynthia seemed quite keen to get them out from under her feet while she cooks the tea, but they haven't showed. Maybe I should go round and collect them – I hadn't thought, but Sidney and Lloyd are too young to come out on their own, aren't they? And their dad Harold won't be home from work yet.'

'Lloyd is only four – maybe too young to come at all, Alan?'

'Yeah, do you mind if I pop round, though? It won't take me long – they live just round the corner and I feel bad about them. I hate to think of them in that hostel… Plank wheezing away in the damp little rooms…'

'Go, it's a good idea. We won't get started for a little while and the first week is really just to get them together and give them a feel for it. And Ricci's here now anyway.'

Ricci is striding over the grass, pulling a ladies' shopping trolley.

'Hello, hello all and sundry. Refreshments I bring!'

It might seem unusual that any of these children can come out into the streets of Central London on their own. But this is their home, their 'manor' and they still do get out, though less than generations past, I suppose. They all know their way to the square, because, in a quaint, incongruous touch, evocative of more suburban after -school streets, it's where the ice-cream van stops each day, when school's out.

Before his tumble, I've gathered, Ali knew his way around best of all. Every shop keeper knows him and the family has been showered with goodwill grocery provisions since his accident, Mrs Oppah tells me. He had liked to lurk in the back of their shops, messing about on their computers. What had he done there, what was the attraction, I wonder?

Stuffing his face with crisps, Sylvie.

84

'Fantastic, Ricci. Thanks. So far it's mainly primary school age, but I was hoping…'

'… Hello Sylvie, we're here! Didn't want to miss your first lesson.'

'Rejoice and Philomena! Hello. And is that Ana by the bikes?'

'Yep. She only come because she might get to see her boyfriend. He's a chef in that place over there.'

I wave at Ana, who waves back. Tiny body you might mistake for a railing, huge grin.

The children are sitting themselves down on our rugs and beginning to poke at the mannikins.

'These are disgusting, Sylvie.'

'Spooky, like dead babies, innit?'

I can't stop grinning.

'I'm so glad you've come. Its brilliant!'

'It's important.' says Philomena gruffly.

'I need to know what to do when my mum has a fit. I do know, kind of, but… she's been having more lately and I figured this might be the place to learn. Plus, Ana – well, she needs someone to keep an eye on her.'

Rejoice is smiling. 'And my dad said it would be good for me to know some tips for when my brothers and sisters get to England. Younger children can be accident prone, my dad said.'

An implausibly handsome man in chef whites has appeared at Ana's side. They sit down together on the steps by the railing.

'Your mum's fits have got more frequent Phil?'

'Yeah, but no big deal, Sylvie, yeah? Don't make a fuss of it.'

'Okay. We will cover first aid for fits, of course. But not today, so maybe we can talk next week at school, Phil?'

'Maybe, if I've got time. Are we going to get this training underway though? I haven't got all night!'

'Right.'

The children are all gathered on the rugs, chatting and playing with the baby manikins. Ricci and Nelly sit in their midst, Ricci having handed out squash and a biscuit to each child. Maybe the squash should have come later.

I cannot quite believe they are here, that a tiny, old fashioned public health initiative has actually worked thus far. They all look up expectantly...

'Okay guys... now in First aid there are lots of acronyms, that means initials for things, but really there is only one that you all need to know. It will become so familiar to you, that you could recite it in your sleep, and we're going to start with that, base all our learning on that and come back to it again and again, or whenever we are unsure. First aid is all about practice.'

And so we begin, with the fantastically unprepossessing acronym in all its glory. D.R.A.B.

'Wouldn't B.A.R.D be better,' heckles Ricci, for whom letter order has no firm construct. 'After all, it is Shakespeare's 400th birthday this week.'

'Death day,' corrects Kayleigh. 'Its 400 years since he died, not got born. Don't you know nothing? And what's a bard?'

'It's both, Kayleigh. Shakespeare's birthday was the same as his death day. No, it needs to be D.R.A.B, I'm afraid. You'll see why. By the way, guys, for those of you who don't know, this is Dr Ricci Jones and I'm Sylvie, you know me. Alan, who many of you also know, is coming along in a minute.'

'You a proper doctor?' asks Jai.

'Nope. Not at all, darlings. I'm a doctor of sexual health.'

'A sex doctor,' muses Ali.

'Don't be fucking disgusting, Ali,' says Jai.

'Maybe we should do introductions first, Sylvie?' says Ricci.

'Of course we should,' I say. 'I'm so excited to see you all, I'm getting carried away.'

And so we introduce ourselves, with our ages, Sheena's idea: Ricci (fifty-five), Sylvie (fifty) Jai (twelve), Ali (eleven), Sheena (ten) Kayleigh (eleven), Rejoice (fourteen), Philomena (fifteen), and the four from All Saints, all aged eleven.

'Ana, sixteen, is still over there with lover boy,' says Philomena.

'That's fine. It will be good for us to show our learning by repeating to her what we know when she does come. What about your friend over there, Kayleigh?'

'He ain't my friend.' Then, 'Oi! Coming over?!' she shouts at a terrifying pitch.

But the boy shrugs and turns away, moving fast away from the park now.

'Baby.' says Ali, inexplicably.

As we are getting towards the end of the introductions, Alan arrives, just in time to introduce himself, Alan (twenty-six), Plank (twelve), Angus (eight), Sydney (six) and Lloyd (four).

'Plank! Plank What sort of a name is that?' starts Kayleigh.

'And ground rules,' Alan interjects.

'Thank you, Alan for reminding us. We don't need many, this isn't school, but a few basic principles and the main ones will be kindness and respect for each other, Kayleigh. Got it?'

Kayleigh nods, chewing her nail now.

'An' if it rains can we go in Shakespeare's house?', she gesticulates to the mock tudor grotto. 'He lived there y' know. And died there.'

I pick one of the armless, legless, clumsily constructed to appear ethnically inclusive child dummies and lie it on the grass in front of them;

'So, imagine you came out of your house, or flat or whatever, one morning and found this boy, let's call him…'

'Ali!'

'Okay, let's call him Ali, lying in the middle of the road. Your instinct is to help him, of course, but what's the very first thing you would need to think about?

'Why his head is half black, half white.'

'Why he's got no arms and legs.'

'Those things, of course, my manikins have limitations – you'll need to use your imagination in First Aid, but what else, before you rush out to help him?'

When I'm teaching adults on Saturday mornings, it often feels rushed. Their precious Saturday hours and mine slip away so tricksy fast and there is so much knowledge to impart. My method, aiming for cognitive, kinesthetic or whatever, can become increasingly behavioural, as I rattle through the hideous menu of potential disasters that comprises the Ofsted paediatric requirement, against the clock. However well

I have prepared, it is just me telling and them listening, squeezing in the horrors of meningitis and fast-onset conditions at the end, before a quick recap on the practicalities of cardio-pulmonary resuscitation. Today, I realise with a rush of euphoria, need not be that way. We can take our time. We can spend a whole session on 'DANGER' – the first concept in the all-important acronym. We can even spend the whole time on the importance of considering DANGER TO OURSELVES first and this will be time well spent. Providing they come back, of course. But even if they don't, really. It's up to us how fast we go, what pace we take and everything in first aid is useful, that we know.

In fact they are quicker than my adult learners, their mixed ages and ability only an asset really, as these concepts are deliberately simple. Of course they swiftly comprehend that it would be stupid to run into the road and risk getting knocked down by a car.

'Or to jump into a lake without looking for a lifebelt. Or, can anyone think of another example?'

'Or to forget to look up from your dinner when fat pig Ali is falling from the sky!'

'Kayleigh,' warns Alan.

Ali beams, Plank and his siblings huddled on the rug next to Nelly, look alarmed. Plank fingers his inhaler.

By the end of a happily passing hour, in which they and indeed Alan, Ricci, Nelly and I seem properly engaged with our learning, they are all pumping away on the manikins, executing erratic CPR. We attract some attention from passers-by and pigeons, but no one pesters.

'What are we doing next week, Sylvie?'

'Let's just recap – DRAB stands for;

'DANGER, RESPONSE, AIRWAY, BREATHING!!' they chorus in unison.

'Brilliant! And next week, in answer to your question, Plank, we are going to learn about the next 'B'. Any ideas?'

'Broken bones?'

'No, broken bones are significant if they happen to you.'

'Like me!'

'Yes, like you, Ali. But they are seldom life threatening. Another B?'

'Bumming.'

'Ashley... ',

And on for a bit, until they get 'Bleeding' and we let them go, with a final reminder that what they are learning is true first aid. Everything done by paramedics after that is a mere *second, third or fourth*. Alan walks Plank and his brothers home. Lloyd has appropriated one of the baby manikins and is keen to hang on, so we let him take it home with him.

As we are packing up, Ana rushes up.

'Sorry Sylvie. I got caught up with... him' she smiles her ravishing smile, gesturing back over to the railings.

'Has Philomena gone?'

'I'm here. You so aren't going learn any First Aid carrying on over there with *him*, are you? We done loads'

'Yes, sorry. He's... it just happened to be his tea, well fag, break.'

'Don't worry Ana. We can show you what we learnt next week. It's been fun.'

'Come on then, stupid,' says Philomena, linking arms with Ana.

'You know I've got to get back to mum. You can tell me about him on the way home. She lives in the next door block to me, Sylvie. See ya. Bye Dr Ricci. You had better teach Ana some of your sex health if she keeps seeing that chef guy.'

'Phil. Shut up!'

'You coming an' all, 'Joice?'

We watch them head off in the Oxford Street direction.

'What complete dears, Sylvie.' Ricci wipes his brow. 'I adore them. For once we are actually teaching them something useful, too. And they enjoyed it. They need more food though. Rejoice and Plank and his brothers were properly hungry. What's their story?'

'Rejoice is a refugee, Plank and his family live in a hostel.'

'Ah ,I felt a bit like Jesus in the loaves and fishes, except the food ran out. Suffer the little children. Maybe we could get unsold sandwiches from E.A.T or Neros for next week.'

'Thanks so much Ricci. You were great. You look a bit tired.'

'I'm fine and dandy. I knew I should have been a school nurse.'

'Glory would be proud of us, wouldn't she?'

'Hmm. Thought I saw her earlier.'

'Ricci!'

'No, truly. Just out of the corner of my eye, you know. Nelly noticed too – over there on the bench, chuckling to herself, then gone. What? I mean it's not so weird, Sylvie, don't look at me like that. If Glory were to be anywhere it would be here, surely, among the flowers, resting on the bench a while, approving of us being with these kids. She was wearing…'.

'Maybe. Let's take all this lot in now, its clouding over. We've been so lucky with the weather.'

I'm resorting to weather talk. I don't tell Ricci that I've heard Glory in the hall,

But I'm privately relieved that it is not just me who hears and sees the unsurprising and unexplainable, for there is another little story waiting in the wings, like a half remembered dream or one still to be dreamt. Alice and her talk of Norwich mystics has reminded me. Something slightly strange that happened at the beginning of this academic year and got me thinking back to our school days, that time when we make transition from years six to seven. Back then we call it 'Fourth Year' at primary and inexplicably 'Upper Three' at the new school.

I was driving up to Cromer from London, snatching a few last spare summer days, when work was quiet and nobody would miss me in London. The early evening was still with a westerly, warm air. When you are a busy working person there is not much time for contemplation, but time alone in a car can be that time. Don't all adults love time driving alone?

'Welcome to Norwich. A fine city.'

The famously assertive sign I remembered with affection, from growing up round there. Norwich is right to declaim her fineness, I can see that now, could even then. She is a very fine city. This sign, placed at all entry points, is made of metal, with a painting of the cathedral spire rising behind the lettering.

'Not such a fine city if you have to go to school there every day.'

We used to grumble away happily, on our way in each morning from our small village ten miles west, in one or another of our mothers' cars. Sometimes the fathers would drive us in, mine particularly because as a vicar he kept less ordered work hours than other peoples' dads. But usually it was one of our mothers; often cross, preoccupied, busy with a million things as mothers are.

'Your mum's pretty.' said Finn.

'Is she? Yours is prettier.'

A disloyal retort, but it hadn't actually occurred to me to consider the mums as pretty or otherwise until we started this new school. Mums were over thirty and that was old, really. But now I began to notice their brown legs, bare arms, damp natural hair from a rushed early start. They were still youthful, I supposed, with life and some love still left in them. Was the object of their love our dads? This seemed too improbable to contemplate, so we would glide swiftly back to our eleven-year-old worlds, our own preoccupations, storing small glimmers of pre-understanding. I expect the mothers relished their journeys home after dropping us off. The peace of it.

I had reached the inevitable traffic jam at the top of the A11 coming into town this evening. Should I go down through the elegant, tree-lined Newmarket Road, past my old school and through the city, or round the expedient ring road? I took the road through the beautiful old city, for me so evocative of my own school days, but with her churches and castle and cathedral and walls, a mystic place for any age. Then out the other side on the old Norwich road, thinking how, nearly forty years since my school days our memories can be so sharp, intense and modern, as though not memories at all, but part of a continuum.

The half-remembered aspect of that evening had to do with Mother Julian and her Norwich world. She had been on my mind lately, even before Alice brought her up.

'All shall be well and all shall be well and all manner of things shall be well' is a comforting phrase at the very least, for a modern person. And 'serious respect', as my children say, for a woman who made such a mark in her own time, that her comforting words resonate so strongly now. Sitting in the traffic, cut off from my life for a little time, I contemplated the contemplative life from a very safe distance.

We learnt about Mother Julian in that first term of big school, beginning in around the third week when life still felt like late summer, not early autumn. Our head mistress, a scholarly person who I later admired hugely but then… has an eleven-year-old even learnt how to appraise what they are thinking at all? Adolescent steps still some way off and one foot trailing in the primary school field, what do we think about our own feelings, or others? How much do we contemplate ourselves in the context of our future lives as women or reflect on our shift from childhood as it is happening? Pretty much not at all, then the odd shaft of light, a leap of insight.

'Miss Sheppard's not pretty is she?'

'Not at all. But she is properly old.'

'Yeah. How old, do you think?'

'Fifty, at least.'

Miss Sheppard marched us down through Norwich in crocodile and took the time and trouble to show us our county city in one afternoon. She made the effort to do all that when we were new, which couldn't have been hugely enjoyable for her. I don't remember us being an appreciative audience, but the strange thing is that I recall it now, more distinctly than so much of the years' supposed learning that followed. I remember her scholarly enthusiasm and I remember understanding even then that there was a subtext. Miss Sheppard, not a mother herself, was showing us that there are different ways for women to be in every time; in medieval Norwich, in the late nineteen seventies as we were then. Perhaps now, too in our brave new Millennium.

'Was Mother Julian a mother, Miss Sheppard?'

'She might well have been a wife and mother. She may have had children. Some of her children may even have died in the plague.'

We stomped down Kings Street together, companionably. I do remember thinking that if this is big school, then I liked it. Unfortunately, that day wasn't representative.

We came to a small, city church, tucked away behind the river, stopping in a tidy graveyard with railings.

'We know precious little about her life before she became so ill, saw the Lord manifest in visions and recovered, with a consequent desire to communicate her experience so strong she had to leave all behind and enter a closed order of one.'

We filed into the small, well ordered place, squashed together. So, Norfolk churches were not all wild and vast and full of faded riches like my father's own, then? I tried briefly to envisage what being the vicar of this peaceful, contained place surrounded by city people might entail.

Miss Sheppard moved us into a small priest's hole, a tiny room with a gap in the stone so Mother Julian could have seen out into the chancel and have berries and nuts poked through by kind parishioners, perhaps.

'We have one of these in my father's church,' I blurted out, the other girls looking at me.

'Ah yes, Cawston. You do. Exquisite rood screen and fine hammer beam angels.'

Our headmistress had remembered where I lived! What a thing.

My father worried about the upkeep and the fabric fund, the dwindling congregation and their staid ways, resistant to modern worship. Deep down, in ways I could brush off and away most days, but could not have articulated, I worried about my dad.

'This is more cosy,' I said. Then when she looked at me directly and I was aware of the others staring, added, embarrassed by the word I had chosen;

'I mean more peaceful. Um, prayerful?'

'Cosy is not a bad word, Sylvie. Very cosy, for medieval times and I expect being a woman, she made it just so, before settling down to write her Revelations of Divine Love, having first learned to read and write, of course.'

She paused, staring at her own large feet for a moment, which were solid, in ungainly shoes, with brown tan tights, then continued;

'In fact on reflection, the priest's hole in Cawston is far more authentic than this place as, if memory serves, it is thought to be from 1300, the same century as Julian. This church was almost completely rebuilt after war damage, you see.'

Moving out into the chancel again, she added: 'A special place, Cawston,', with a cursory nod to me that seemed to suggest she might understand another world, my home world before big school, where I could sing in our empty, light barn of a building or climb our tall tower with no hint of a parapet and survey the harvest fields for miles around and feel capable and free and invincible…

As we left the shrine and moved off up towards the cathedral, Miss Sheppard continued to explain that Mother Julian had been remarkable because she didn't run off to France to a Carmelite order or some such, but entered into the religious life right there, in the heart of her Norwich world. She abided in the eye of the storm, while plague and politics raged around her. Kings Street was a hub in those days, not the backwater of riverside warehouses it had become by the 1970s. The city of Norwich ran a different way, river to cathedral the main thoroughfare. Miss Sheppard imparted the idea that in the middle of medieval noise and haste, there could be a place for stillness.

'We owe much of our knowledge about Julian to another important Norfolk woman, Marjory Kempe, who transcribed and saved Julian's work. Interestingly, they wrote about God as both a man and a woman. Extraordinary, heretical concepts for their time. '

Heretical was a word I didn't know, but one of the bright, neat girls whose blue uniform fitted sleekly asked about it and an explanation came. Most of our parents had evidently purchased uniforms to allow for growth. Mine was huge, but then so was I. I seemed to be growing taller before my own eyes, feeling different every day.

In the cathedral, we took turns to look at the carved, painted bosses high in the roof, with the aid of a large mirror on wheels and wandered round some more, while Miss Sheppard told us more interesting and important things, which went over our heads. Then we sat on the grass in the Close, drinking cartons of squash through straws. I was not very surprised to see my own father crossing the grass, with another priest. The cathedral seemed a place where clergymen might gather as a refuge from their parishes, for contemplation together, or retreat. Fathers went on 'retreat' frequently if they were clergy, to contemplate and restore themselves. I am not sure that mothers got time to retreat.

'That's my dad.'

'So it is,' said Miss Sheppard.

My father, deep in conversation, seemed to recognise Miss Sheppard before he noticed me and waved cordially to her, without breaking off his conversation. He moved his hands animatedly as he talked, the other clergyman nodding earnestly.

'Your dad's not bad looking.' one girl said, eyeing him over her straw.

'You think?'

'You look like him.'

'Do I?' I was so surprised by this comment and would have loved to make conversation from it, but I couldn't remember her name. It was so hard to remember any of them, because apart from the very tidy ones, they all looked much the same.

'Hello darling,' Dad said to me, eventually. 'Am I meant to be taking you home?'

'No, Mark. The children will be escorted back to school, unless you want to take her now?' said Miss Sheppard.

I hadn't known they were friends.

Having first a fourteenth century priest's hole and then a priest father to my name, rather elevated me that day, I felt. Later, he was embarrassing as all dads become, and then he had died all of a sudden. But at eleven I just felt happy, skipping off with my hand in his, over the Close to our orange-red Fiat 126.

If Miss Sheppard hoped for great things from me she was to be sadly disappointed. I was not so influenced by important Norfolk women to aspire to become one myself at all, but luckily other girls exceeded expectation in our high achieving girls' school, so I hope she felt fulfilled in her career.

'How do you know Miss Sheppard, Daddy?' I asked as we stuttered home in our little car that sounded like a lawn mower and resembled a baked bean. My tall father had to hunch over the flimsy wheel, but he liked tiny cars for the feeling of adventure.

'Diocesan Synod.'

Two more church words, like so many I was used to hearing, enjoyed the sound of and barely understood.

'She is an impressive scholar, Sylvie. Excavated Mount Masada, stronghold of the zealots.'

'Oh.'

But I wasn't really listening by then. I had wound down the window to breathe in the warm harvest air from the late summer fields. I was wondering about school and hoping that all the things I didn't understand wouldn't matter so much, now Miss Sheppard had seemed to approve of me. Dad was fumbling for his matches to relight his cigarette.

Almost to himself, he added: 'Also a lesbian. A founder member of the recently formed Gay Christian Movement, which is equally impressive in a different way, I suppose.'

I was about to ask what a lesbian was, but that was when the car began to jolt and stutter, before rolling gently to a stop by the side of the road.

'Bugger. We may have run out of petrol.'

And that hadn't been surprising either. Our cars often broke down because they were not new and shining and in this case the petrol dial was inaccurate, with a tank so small that we really needed to fill up most journeys. Petrol was rising to a pound a gallon in 1978 and my father sometimes forgot to fill up, with his mind on higher things. We were used to journeys punctuated by breakdowns.

'Now, where are we?' he asked mildly.

Fields of gold after harvest, no houses, some trees, was all that I could see.

'About a mile from the Marsham garage, I think,' he answered himself.

He leapt out of the car and fetched a small petrol can from the bonnet, which was where our boot was on the Fiat 126.

'Up for a bit of a walk…?'

We had set off together along the Norwich Road, not bothering to lock our Fiat, because who would steal a car with no petrol? A mile wasn't too far, I was thinking, thought it was quite hot and we hadn't any water and then there was the journey back to the car to consider too… My father walked fast with long strides, so I matched his strides, practising for being very tall

'Mark my footsteps good my page,' we were humming, when a long green car pulled up a few yards ahead of us and a lady called out from her driver's window;

'Can I help?'

We stared at the lady, who seemed hazy in the evening sun.

'Do we know her, Daddy?'

'No, I don't think so. Why do you say that?'

'Dunno. She looks a bit familiar.'

'Yes, she does, doesn't she?'

'is she one of the mothers?'

As I remember, the lady had come over to us as we stood, slightly gormlessly in the road. She had grinned, taking in the empty can, then handed us a full one, decisively.

'Hello, you two. I thought that might be the problem. Here, have this.'

She had held out a green plastic can, not unlike ours and handed it to my father, who seemed, for once, lost for words.

'I always carry a spare these days, just in case, you know?' she said.

My dad reached out for her petrol can, starting to recover himself to speak, but the lady just grinned again, appraising me and my father affectionately, before turning quickly to walk back to her own car, with long strides.

When she reached her car, she gave a friendly wave.

'So good to see you both. Take care' she called… And then drove fast away, disappearing over a small Norfolk hill.

So my father and I only had to walk back five minutes to our car and the petrol from the lady's oil can saw us easily home.

My father and I were silent on the last bit of our journey back to the village, but when he had stopped in our rectory drive and pulled on the creaking hand break, he put his hand over mine and looking straight ahead said: 'No sure what happened there, Sylvie.'

'No.'

'I mean, something did, but I'm not sure quite what.'

He had looked at me, with his small blue eyes that I have, that maybe the lady had, too.'

'She was quite pretty, wasn't she, Daddy?'

'She was.'

'And she wasn't one of the mothers, was she?'

'I don't think she was, no.'

'But she helped us.'

'She did.'

He held my hand in his big hand for one more second or so.

'Sylvie, don't worry. Everything needn't be explained.'

'I'm not worried, Dad.'

And about that I didn't worry. We had climbed out of our hot little car and gone in for supper, keeping what happened between ourselves.

Driving out of Norwich that evening last September, I passed the battered Fiat 126 on the road, a beat before I had known I would. And then minutes later a tall man in dog collar holding a petrol can, walking along the dusty road with a girl in blue school uniform, do you see? And that happened, which is strange because it couldn't have, quite. I called out, gave them the can which I always keep with me because you never know. And for a short second or two was so very pleased to see them standing on the road together, before I drove fast away. I looked to see them in my rear view mirror, but they had gone, or I had driven over a small Norfolk hill.

Then, like my father and earlier self I thought best not to mention such a thing, until I talked to Theo.

'You go back and you meet your younger self on the road. Is that so strange?,' said Theo.

'And my father?'

He smiled.

'And your lovely father. How did they look?'

'They looked... it was lovely to see them. Good to be able to help them.'

'How lucky that was, then Sylvie? Don't worry. Everything need not be explained.'

Chapter Eight

In Piccadilly Primary, a few polluted streets from Soho Square, a curious phenomenon is affecting one clever, beautiful girl. You will know my narrative well enough already to know that I consider them all clever and beautiful, all these darling babes we have the privilege to be alongside. Particularly those in the summer term of their Year six. It's not just me, it's as though we all – every teacher, office manager, dinner supervisor and caretaker, all melt with a strange nostalgia in action:

'Ah, I remember when they were little scraps who could hardly tie their shoe laces and now look at them...'

'his chubby little face in nursery...'

'How she used to cry every day when her mum left her...'

And look at them, indeed; at the top of the school these eleven-year-olds are growing into themselves as they grow out of their baby schools. They can be proud and dignified, the boys and girls even get on with each other and begin to find buds of attraction in each other that will blossom, flourish, wither, perish and begin again time and time over, in the next few years. There is a competence about these gracious young people at the top of their school that will vanish when they appear in their new establishments two months hence. Their head teachers give them responsibilities, like mentoring the younger ones, or running the library. Shiny metal medals adorn their proud chests: LIBRARY MONITOR, SCHOOL COUNCIL REP, SECRETARY

OF STATE FOR EDUCATION… Everything is possible from these extraordinary people. They believe it. And so do we. They have their SATS to sit and once sat, let them enjoy their summer in the sun. It is a term of promise, a time of expectation.

But for Pearl at Piccadilly Parish, South West of the square, life doesn't look this way. Something is not right, all is not well and we're not sure why.

'Let's go over the symptoms again, Alan.'

'Symptoms isn't a word you use much, Sylvie.'

'No, sorry. I should be more nursey.'

'I suppose it's because we are working with the healthy population and to a social model, rather than medical. I suppose it's about looking at the whole healthy child?'

'Maybe. I'm definitely becoming more psychologically minded. Maybe I need to be brought back to basics.'

'Oh, I dunno, "the unexamined life…and all that".'

"Her symptoms are vague, panic attacks really, I wonder what causes them…?"

And on we chat until we're at the front door of school, juniors' entrance.

'The fear of the Lord is the beginning of wisdom…'. I hadn't noticed that before. Not very welcoming, is it?'

Alan is reading the Victorian benefactors' stern inscription carved into the stone above our heads.

'The infants' door has "Suffer the little children to come unto me".'

'Better, I guess.'

"Kind of."

104

I wonder if Alan will stay in our team when he qualifies at the end of the summer. He is so easy to talk to and a natural sounding board for my more random thoughts and ideas. I'll miss him hugely if he leaves, but he may prefer to work nearer his home and any Trust would snap him up. I don't ask, dreading his answer. Still, it's only May. It is still but a baby elephant in the room.

We spend the morning organising a referral to the play therapist, for Pearl, who had become strangely introvert, having been the life and soul of school and a budding actress. The morning passes swiftly and we are back at the clinic at lunch time.

'Alan opens the door of the clinic and we are back in our hall of dreams. A refreshing breeze blows from nowhere.

'Transition, moving on, changing schools, changing body. Year Six isn't a breeze for everyone, is it, Sylvie?'

I press the lift button. It's only one floor down to our basement, but I love this old fashioned wooden lift with a latticed inside door that concertinas. I seldom take the stairs.

Being the broker for other services is an important and sometimes underrated part of our role as school nurses. I know that with Lucy the play therapist, the young girl Pearl, who loves acting and has suddenly become shy will feel safe to explore her muddles, or not, as she decides. She won't be pushed or forced, but there will be space for her, a therapeutic space to be. We can't push parents either, or pretend that therapy is something it's not. But for Pearl, a play may turn the key to the secret garden.

'For Pearl, a therapeutic space to play might just help. This may sound weird, but I get the strong feeling that she is scared of leaving childhood behind. Does that sound silly?'

'Nothing you say sounds silly. You are very sound in your judgement. Let's put our faith in play therapy.'

105

As I leave the clinic after work and move onto Berwick Street, the market traders are packing up their stalls for the day, but one stops me;

'Sign our petition to save our street?'

'I've signed already, but happy to do so again, if it helps.'

'Thanks love. Two hundred years we've been here. We've got millions of signatures, but the bastard council's only giving us ' til end of June before our licenses our cut. It's not all posh gits here, you know. Some of our customers are in their nineties and come to us for their milk and veg, you know? Then there's the little kiddies running errands for their mums. Oh, wait a minute, you're the school nurse from Soho Square, aint yah? I don't need to tell you about community and kids. You're teaching my Ashely First Aid! He's dead enthusiastic about that. And the sex stuff you taught them, not meaning to be rude, that was helpful, that was. Saved me a job! 'Ere Alf, it's the school nurse.'

'I'm glad Ashley likes the sessions. I'm guessing all the building work round here will be affecting your trade too? The road's been blocked from both ends for months, by lorries and trucks. No one can get in. And then there's the high speed rail digging!'

'You're not wrong, nurse. I'ts them fucking trucks and brick dust and noise. Not "building work" though nurse, it's a demolition mob. They're destroying old Soho from the inside out they are, soon they'll be nuffink left. The Berwick Street Blitz, they's calling it! And who needs bombs when you've got that high speed rail link flattening everything we knew and loved.'

And yes, they really do speak like that. And yes, their market stalls could be from the set of Oliver on Drury Lane, And yes, the metaphors are obvious and all around us; it's all about cleansing and privatising in the name of progress, in our health service and in the streets of London alike.

I walk on home, under a canopy of pale green, early summer plane trees.

Hello Finn. How is it going?

Argh. Hello! Not waving but drowning, me, in a sea of parish bureaucracy. Huge amounts of good will from all the volunteers – practical help too – we have been given some lovely old furniture from a primary school, that only needs a lick of paint. We even have paint donated from the Norwich Fired Earth... very posh, and a magnificent coffee machine and a crepe maker and endless crockery, though some is more crock than china. But there are still some obstacles. The Facebook campaign is in full swing, have you seen? I feel so stuck though! Something has to shift. But what? When? Help Sylvie! We are too far away from each other. Come back soon please... half-term holiday? How are you? How's Dr Ricci and the teamlet, those dear babes and their first aid lessons? Will you teach us first aid in the summer, if we ever open?

And that silly goose is still sitting in the tree.

I cross Birdcage Walk, past The Westminster Arms and here is the Abbey again, our man-made mountain of a thousand years. Like a mountain it looks different in every light and this evening the stone is dusty pink.

You might be nearly there, Finn; always darkest before the dawn and other crap clichés, you know? Btw do geese ever nest in a tree?

Something will shift soon in Cromer, I feel it in my bones. Westminster council and the Berwick Street traders may be less lucky. Our lovely, grubby old Soho may fade away like an insubstantial pageant.

Never heard of such a thing in a goose. *But I will check with the hen man who's promised to provide free eggs for our community cakes. If we ever get to open... love you. How is school nursing?*

The sun is setting on school nursing.

Oh fine, you know.

Hey! Sylvie!

Can't explain.

Okay. Write it down.

Trying...

Change and shifting patterns. I have tears pricking as I move into Dean's Yard. There is a blackbird pulling out all the stops in a highest branch, competing with the Abbey organ on one side and the cacophony of choristers' random music practice half hour on the other. The new leaves move gently and a timeless light falls across the green. I think of those fledglings in Year Six, take a deep breath and run home across the grass.

Chapter Nine

We are moving swiftly through summer term now. The beloved Year sixes finished their all-important SATs exams this week and can now begin to focus on the fun times. First aid gathers pace; with a remarkable low attrition rate and impressive tenacity, the learners now have a competent working knowledge of the drab but essential DRAB, as well as a gratifying understand of not just what we do for Bleeding, Burns and Broken Bones, but *why*. Alan Ricci and I feel proud of them all and are moving on to the first aid for other conditions. If we had stuck to the strictest order, Philomena would have had to wait too long to learn how to look after her mum when she is fitting, and Ashley wouldn't have known how to care for his street trader dad who, it turns out, is a newly diagnosed diabetic and prone to hypos. But we have that greatest of all luxuries – time, with no deadline, other than the possibility that the lessons become boring and people stop turning up. So we can jump and flit from seizures to diabetes, to sickle cell to meningitis, hypothermia to heat stroke, nosebleeds to poisoning and we can begin and end our every session with CPR. Even Sydney and Lloyd have a passable technique at baby resuscitation. And all our babies recover, so Lloyd can line them up and feed them biscuits if the talk gets too technical.

They love scenarios best, the grizzlier the better, school coach crash, high school massacre... they divide themselves into victims or rescuers and launch into enthusiastic rescue missions. This has evolved as the second half of every session, the first half being where we teach them a new principle.

'They really *get* Shock, now don't they?' Ricci says, impressed as we watch Plank and Philomena tending to Ana's convincingly bloodless form. Ana graces us with her presence only when her chef can't take a fag break. He seems to take several an hour. Plank gently raises her legs, while Philomena applies direct pressure to an imaginary wound, elevating her injured arm.

'It's like her body's a radiator, remember what Sylvie said,' Phil bosses,

'The pressure's gone low, because she's leaking from somewhere, so we bring her feet up slightly to get the blood back to her heart and we apply direct pressure here.'

'But what if she's bleeding internally? She looks like she's losing blood fast, look at her pale face. Sylvie! What if she's got internal injuries? Can't remember… Alan, help!'

Alan moves over, ever patient, ever sure, to help.

Kayleigh is sorting some old bandages we have been donated, by the district nurse team in our clinic. She looks across at Ali, Philomena and Plank.

'What if she's been stabbed?' she says quietly

'Good point, Kayleigh.' We do need to cover stabbing injuries. Next week, remind me?'

'May be too late.'

'What did you say?'

'Nothing.'

Sometimes Plank's parents come along and sit on the bench while we teach. They both look exhausted and preoccupied, but have had news recently of a flat they may be able to move to.

'It's in Barking though, Sylvie.'

'Barking's okay, Harold.'

'Miles away. Plank's father gazes across the grass miserably, as though he might see Barking in the middle distance.'

'I've lived round here all my life, since my parents came over. Never further than Camden. Makes me feel bad I cannot provide for the family here in the heart of our beautiful city. And that hostel, Sylvie...', he shakes his head solemnly.

'...Not good, not good. Have you been inside?'

I haven't, but Alan has reported back, from his trips to pick up the children and deliver them home. Cockroaches and grime in the corridors, one bathroom for every floor of rooms and an impenetrable metal door, outside which men who look old and are probably not at all, sit with cider cans and dried up paper coffee cups for half- hearted begging.

'It's damp too, which is so bad for Plank's asthma. I feel so ashamed that this is what my family is brought to.'

And I feel ashamed of our country that in these times families should have to live this way, in one of the wealthiest capital cities in the world.

It makes you feel angry Sylvie?

It does, Theo, yes. And powerless.

'His asthma is much better now he has his inhalers sorted and the weather is warming up. Maybe this fresh air is doing him good too?'

'We love Soho Square now, Sylvie. I bring the boys out every afternoon when school's out, to get them out from under Cynthia's feet.'

'If you don't mind me asking Harold – why did you call him Plank?'

'Its short for Plankton.'

Hardly better.

'We named him after a Dr Plankton back home, whom my mother revered.'

Ali Oppah is out of his thick leg cast and into a lighter, pale blue splint. His arm is now free from the plaster altogether and his physio has been firm about exercise, so he makes some effort to wheel himself across the square to our sessions, Jai and Sheena close on his tail. Mrs Oppah comes too now, bringing honey buns for the children, the 'after-picnic' having grown to be quite a thing.

'Surely you wouldn't call these ones buns, Sylvie?' says Ricci, examining one.

'They look great, but why is everything a bun to you? Mrs Oppah, what are these ones called ….'

'She calls them some fucking thing in our language you'll never be able to pronounce it, Ricci.'

'Jai. Not swearing please, in front of the little ones, and don't be rude about your lovely mother.'

Jai is our star first aider though, channeling all her fury at the world into chest compressions, stopping to mop her brow, gulp some squash. But she is also thirsty for knowledge, has memorised the First Aid Made Easy booklet we provide for them all and Ricci has taken to bringing her articles from nursing journals.

'Its all about the evidence-base, Jai. And that is constantly changing, never still.' Ricci explains.

Jai looks unimpressed;

'Yeah? It says here that people who receive bystander CPR are twice as likely to survive to 30 days. I'd want to survive longer than that! Hardly worth the bother!'

'Not all of them get someone tending to them with a technique as good as yours,' Ricci says, beaming proudly at her.

'Can we get an AED or defibrillator to practice with, or whatever they're called? It's says here they make a big difference to outcomes. What's an "outcome"?'

'I've been wondering about getting an AED from somewhere too, Jai,' says Alan.

'Ricci, do you think the NHS might fund one?'

Ricci looks deflated. I've noticed that mention of the wider NHS has a deflating effect on us all these days, casts a gloomy shadow. He rallies quickly for Jai. 'Oh, I don't see why not. There is a nice guy who does all our staff emergency first aid training and re-stocking of equipment. He's a paramedic, Tony. I'll talk to him. Also, we could ask them when they come on their visitation.'

Word of our informal sessions has reached the Powers That Be in our Trust now, thanks to positive feedback from Alice, Will and other head teachers at their monthly joint meeting. There is a move to make it an 'official pilot project', for larger 'roll out', with a timely recent announcement from the Resuscitation Council UK that all school children should be taught CPR and how to use an automated external defibrillator. We are, perhaps by accident, but more probably because we are close to the ground and to community need, 'on message'. In all my years in school nursing, I have first learnt and then taught as sacred principles, the public health premise that interventions need to be evaluated from the planning stage, the evidence-base considered, service users involved and validated tools employed. I'm aware that school nursing has suffered from a lack of such evaluated projects. Recently, the Chief Medical officer referred to the evidence-base for the effectiveness of school nursing as 'small and weak'. Harsh, but she is on our side and she is right. School nursing, as all public health nursing, is under threat because it is hard to quantify the impact of what we do. We do so many different things in different places and arguably all under the broad brush of 'public health interventions'. Sometimes good outcomes may take years to manifest themselves and thorough longitudinal studies are the most expensive of all. So I know we should be using every opportunity to capitalise on initiatives such as this one, to save our service. But I find my heart sinking now the Powers are waking up to our little idea. I see the gleam in their eye that I've seen before, when an intervention they have had no time or money for initially, takes hold and gathers pace naturally. We started our first aid club because local children asked for it. We found a place to be and we involved local children of all ages. In a short time, the group has grown to be a special haven of sorts, for an oddball assortment of kids and for this time in space it meets a need. Someone is coming down from Headquarters to see us in action soon and I find myself dismayed by the prospect. The group occupies only two hours of our working week, negligible resources and planning, but we are aware that strictly speaking we are using Trust time, in a way they may justifiably prohibit, if they so decide. There will be talk of inequity in service delivery; suggestions that similar interventions are offered to all school age children in our borough and beyond. Impossible targets will be imposed and we will, as so often, be set up to fail. Daphne and Chloe influenced me in this dilemma years ago, when I was on the school nursing degree course.

'You can't have complete equity, you can't do everything, so go where there is an opportunity of excellence, they advised. Follow that, using the principles of social capital – build, bridge and link. Then write up and disseminate your small project perfectly, as an example of best practice for others to follow.'

Ricci, Alan and I have made a 'baseline assessment' of all the children's first aid ability and are continuing to monitor their progression, we measure the popularity of our intervention quantitatively, by the numbers that turn up each week (a consistent core of twenty, with a few hangers on) and qualitatively by little questionnaires around how much they like it, how much they feel they're learning.

Help with collecting and analysing this data has come unexpectedly, from a serendipitous source – Sonny, the SCPHN student. Though her own school nursing placement is in South London, it transpires that she lives in Chinatown, where both parents run a Chinese restaurant and that she herself went to Piccadilly Primary.

So actually, I wasn't just being unconsciously biased, she is Chinese.

Well, you were Mum, but this time you happened to be right about her ethnicity, that's all.

Sonny, ever on the search for health needs, had been chatting to Alan at college and when he mentioned the group, asked if she could help in any way.

'She's crazily clever and incredibly enthusiastic about it all. Out of my league.' says Alan.

'Nonsense, you're clever too, Alan!'

'That wasn't what I meant.'

'Tell her "yes" of course, Alan. It would be wonderful to have her on board. She can help us evaluate constructively, measure the impact of our intervention.'

'But basically its just about having a fun time after school, isn't it?' says Ricci as we watch them collapsed and laughing on the grass, after a particularly gruesome motorway pile-up.

'Blah, blah, blah and bollocks to the effective evidence-base.'

'Thus speaks Dr Ricci Jones, *sorry doctor Ricci...*'

'Yes, alright Alan, I'm setting a bad example, sorry. Its important, vital. Maybe I'm just a tired old fuck. Whoops, sorry Jai, you didn't hear that. Swearing is not okay, Jai, not okay.'

'Yeah, yeah, whatever,' says Jay. 'I think it's starting to rain. Can we go into the Shakespeare house?'

'No. Its locked and it's not ours.'

We clear up hurriedly then, rushing all the manikins, blankets and damp buns back over into our grey green hospital hall of dreams. Mrs Oppah acts as lollipop lady as we cross the square, Plank's parents shelter with the little ones under Shakespeare's house, until the rain has eased off enough for them to go 'home', to the hostel.

'Wooah, this place is spooky,' says Jai looking around the hall, surrounded by the dripping manikins she has unceremoniously dropped on the marble floor.

'Is it an old hospital or something?' Full of ghosts, I'm thinking. Who's that calling out?'

Ricci and I look at each other. It's quiet and we can only hear the rain outside and street sounds.

'Funny you should say that, Jai. Anyway, thanks for helping. Do you want to shelter here or will you be off?'

Jai pauses by the door, looks up the stairs, as though she hears someone.

'Nah, no way. I'm out of here guys. I'll go home with mum and the little ones.' She turns to leave.

'Not that Ali is little, eh? The sooner he is up and about and using energy again, the better. I'm gonna get him running up them fucking stairs, I am, Hope he doesn't have a heart attack! Kind of hope he does. Ha! Sort the de-fib, yeah, Ricci? See yah.'

She shuts the door and we are left, waiting for our old fashioned lift.

'What do you think she heard, Ricci?'

'Who, you mean,' Ricci is smiling. 'I think we know.'

'Ricci, I don't want the Powers to come and "visit" us.'

'Nope. Me neither.'

'They may unintentionally spoil it, destroy our intervention by their well-meaning intervening. After all, it's as you said – it's kids having some fun after school and we are helping to facilitate that. Does everything have to be quantified?'

'I know, it's all "what are the measurable outcomes of this intervention?" Kiss of death. It's been a happy summer term diversion, useful for these very children and their families, maybe one day, you never know, some random collapser might benefit from Jai's tremendous resuscitation skill. Basta, enough! But let's not worry. Let's just see where it all takes us, shall we? Here for a season and all that.'

The lift arrives and we pile in the bedraggled manikin babies.

On my way home Finn texts;

Is it an Egyptian goose in the tree?

How would I tell?

'Bird man says white head, big brown eye.'

Yes!

I had just passed mother goose, still perching, in the natural hollow of a curly twisted tree, opposite Duck Island and the little Swiss Chalet.

Not unusual for them to nest in holes in mature trees, parkland trees. Take a photo for me, Sylvie? You were right, by the way – sands shifting in this parts...

Tell!

Soon, Sylvie, soon...

Chapter Ten

'She's well enough to audition? That amazing!'

'Audition? she is practically running the show. Directing, singing along and dancing freely and yes, she got her dream role of Potiphar's wife'.

Lucy, the play therapist and I are conferring in the playground at the start of school. Everyone has gone in to lessons, including Pearl, who is evidently restored now to her thespian self.

'But that's incredible. Its only been a few weeks. How did she make the shift, do you think?'

'I know. And... I don't know, Sylvie. We have been working together on the transition from childhood to adolescence, the fears it holds balanced against the excitement and infinite possibility. There doesn't seem to be any more sinister underlying reason. But her confidence is soaring now.'

'Thank goodness we could refer to you. We were all a bit at sea with her.'

'I'm grateful for the referral and to school nursing for that. We have a place and a space to work through things gently together, but in all seriousness Sylvie, you shouldn't underestimate the importance of your own interaction. Not just the referral. You and Alan were far more than merely brokers for another service. It was you – I don't know quite how – who helped the big shift occur. Pearl was stuck and completely nonplussed by herself.'

'Will Simpson held the purse strings and is empathetic, thank goodness, but it was Pearl's time with you and Alan that may have helped her most because you were open to her and opened the door for our opportunity.'

'Have the bell went, Miss?'

Lucy and I look down to see a breathless child, tie askew, pale, sweating face. I silently applaud his syntax, recognising him as the chipper little boy who had been kicking a ball around with Kayleigh, under the Wardour Street flats that day. He had hovered round First Aid in the initial weeks, but always flitted off, other fish to fry. I had forgotten to ask Kayleigh about him recently. He looks different today. Older, anxious, his eyes darting.

'Oh, hello there. The bell has just gone, I'm afraid.'

He sighs, rubs his face.

'Shit. I'll be late again.'

'Don't worry.' Lucy looks at him kindly, cradling her coffee mug

'Don't worry, its only just gone. I'm sure if you explain why you were late…'.

But the boy shakes his head as though to say 'you have no idea' and runs in.

'Wait, what's your name? We met…' I ask, but he has gone.

'Do you know him, Lucy?'

'That little chap? No. But I tend to only know the ones I'm referred. Where were we? Oh yes, I was saying how important, how vital school nurses are, Sylvie, as that first point of contact who families trust, so that our referrals have a chance of actually sticking, but also for your own sensitive and empathetic work. Does that aspect of school nursing get evaluated? It is hugely underrated in my view.'

'Funny you should say that…'.

119

I feel intensely grateful for Lucy's affirmation and make a mental note to talk to Ricci, Alan, Daphne and Chloe, Sonny... all of them, because evaluating our own interventions properly and not overlooking is of course what matters, what makes the difference. It would be interesting to analyse the sundry benefits of meeting for first aid - check if the course learning objectives were enhanced in any way by school nurses running it. But I'm also distracted now; by the delightful image of an all-singing all-dancing, all Joseph seducing Pearl, but also in contrast by the disturbing vision of this distracted boy whose name we don't know. He had looked completely strung out and startlingly unhealthy, as though he had barely seen sunlight, as though he hadn't been 'playing out' much at all. And something else.

He had looked terrified.

Later, in the school office requesting tickets for Joseph, I mention the boy to Will.

'Oh, that's Bailey. Come into my office, Sylvie, where we can speak more privately.'

I follow him in to his little room behind the school office and he shuts the door carefully.

'Bailey Bennett. I was going to refer him back to your service this week actually. He has really nose-dived this term. He lives round the corner in the Berwick Street flats, good friends with Kayleigh and the Oppah children, was quite a promising footballer and very good at maths in school. I should say when he's in school though, now; he has been late most days this term, then recently was off for nine days. Nine! Came back with some half- baked excuse for his absence. I had tried his brother and father and there was always a message left with the office every morning, saying he had tonsillitis, but we never saw a doctor's note. I was pestering his social worker, who had tried to visit, but not gained entry, and then he came back.'

'Family?'

'It's a sad little set up. His dad lives on the other side of the borough. He used to live with his mum and older brother, but his mum died last year. Now he is meant to live with his father, but he prefers to stay this side of town and his brother, who is in his early twenties, is not the ideal carer, shall we say.'

'What did his mum die of? Why haven't we known about him before?'

'I think it was cancer of the liver, but there was a history of drug and alcohol abuse. Bailey was in care for a while when he was much younger, but from Year Three to Five things were fairly stable and mum was clean. His mum got ill very quickly and when she had first died his dad seemed to step up and become quite caring, but that has fallen away and I think his brother is in with a bad lot. He was inside for a while, I think.'

'Social services?'

'Bailey does have a social worker, as I said; you know those families where they have been Child In Need or Child Protection Plan for so long, that we almost take it for granted? I know that's bad.'

'But I do know what you mean.'

'I think you will be hearing from him, as I've called for a professionals meeting this week. The reason you probably haven't got him on your radar is that until his mum died he had been going through a stable time and doing well at school. It's hard, Sylvie. Bailey was a bit of an urchin, but he has always seemed resilient and has a brilliant sense of humour. He is clever, too. He got into a charity boarding school down in Sussex that was founded by the livery companies in Elizabethan times. We had suggested it to his mum as an option after here, she was really keen for him to better himself, so he sat the exam and was all set to go in the autumn, but this term he is elusive and increasingly closed. Grieving, of course, he had a close relationship with his mum and was very protective of her. Lately he has been resistant to offers of help, proud, you know? I am very worried about him. I notice the other kids call him "Baby". A bit like Bailey, I suppose, but a bit odd, because he is the least baby-like child. Worryingly self-sufficient, if anything.'

'I thought he looked frightened, Will, when I saw him just now.'

Will laughs.

'Well, their form teacher can be quite scary when they're persistently late, but I don't think we inspire "the fear of God" in them anymore.'

'Can you fill out a referral form. I'll discuss it with my safeguarding lead and see him asap, if that's okay?'

'Perfect. Oh and your tickets to Joseph are complimentary, naturally. For you, Dr Jones and Alan. Bring the whole team. For years of course, Glory was our school nurse. Remember Glory? She was very much involved with Bailey when he was small. So sad when she departed. She would have loved this production of Joseph.'

And who's to say she won't be there? I don't add.

'Thanks Will.'

***

'Yeah, I know you.'

It is three days later and the first chance I have had to meet Bailey properly. He eyes me warily across the head teacher's desk. I try to move round to be a little nearer him, but he sidles away.

At Piccadilly Primary they always apologise for the lack of regular room, but they, like most of our schools are so pushed for space, we can hardly begrudge them. The head teacher's office is nice in many ways, with a sofa, soft chairs and a large pine desk, but Bailey definitely does not want to be here. He shuffles uncomfortably and looks down at his shoes.

'Nice trainers, Bailey.'

'Yeah, thanks. They're new.'

'Are you okay with my student being here? She is a qualified nurse, training to be a specialist school nurse,'

Sonny is sitting on the opposite corner of the desk. She is with me all week, having done a swap with Alan, so they can both achieve their requisite week of alternative practice. She smiles at Bailey, who gives her a disinterested glance, then looks back to his trainers.

'Yeah. She's okay. Why am I here Sylvie? Am I in trouble? I've been in all week and my brother did a note for when I was off.'

'I know, Bailey. Mr Simpson just asked us to see you to see how you're getting on really, how you are coping since your mum died, how your general health is. You have been through such a lot this past year.'

Bailey looks surprised and his face brightens, as though remembering his mum is not the problem.

'My mum? She was . . . I miss her, I do.'

We talk for a bit about Bailey's mum, using the faithful genogram method to help us picture Bailey's disparate and now diminished family. He gets quite involved, almost despite himself. His sorrow for his mother is palpable and pure.

'And now everything is changed, without her. There's Bradley, who kind of lives with me, in Berwick, then there's my dad who lives mainly in the E Road'

'That's the Edgware Road, Bailey?'

'Yeah, but I don't go up there.'

'Why not? Does your dad come mainly down to you?'

Too many questions, Sylvie. Don't crowd him. Give him a chance to answer and listen, listen to him properly.

A noncommittal 'Yeah.'

You've lost him.

'Why don't you like going up the E Road, Bailey?' asks Sonny, who of course has not lost her train of thought.

But Bailey won't answer that one now either. Why do I feel as though this has become an interrogation? Bailey shuffles uncomfortably on his seat.

'Can I go now?'

Pale, undernourished, with a grubby, grey collar on a tired old uniform. A hole in one sock, his hair lank and long and he is scratching his skin. All the Year Sixes are growing out of their school kit now. No one looks terribly smart at this stage in their primary school career, but Bailey displays some obvious signs of neglect that any half decent school nurse would be familiar with. His new trainers are out of kilter and I don't ask him where he got the money for them, because I already feel we are grilling him.

'Bailey, if there was anything you felt worried about, if anyone is harming you, or if you are harming yourself or anybody else – would you feel able to come to us?'

'Yeah.' But he is looking at his feet again and I have lost him.

Bailey is defending himself

I know, and I feel helpless to reach him. One more try.

124

'You're friends with Kayleigh, aren't you?'

His face brightens again for a moment

'Used to be. When me and Kayleigh was small, people used to think we was twins. But would you call your kids Kayleigh and Bailey? What mother would do that? It's funny because they sound the same, but they're spelt different, see?'

'Were your mum and Kayleigh's mum friends?'

'Yeah. Way back. I wanted to go and live with Kayleigh's mum when my mum died. I was hoping they'd ask me, but they never. Kayleigh's mum, well she works, you know… but I'd of played out with Kayleigh and got my own tea and that. I wouldn't of been no trouble, only company for Kay.'

'Like when I saw you, the day I came to visit Ali. Do you remember, Bailey?'

Bailey looks exactly at me for a moment, as though the memory is a distant one, eclipsed by more recent preoccupations

'Yeah. When Space Hopper fell out the window. Things was different then.' He mumbles wistfully, as though we were talking about years ago, not weeks. And I don't pick him up on this, because I'm aware we have been talking some time and he is missing valuable lessons and because… I can't explain, but I know we are on dangerous territory for Bailey.

'There is a nickname too, isn't there? Baby?'

An inscrutable look passes across his face and he smiles, then shakes his head;

'Nope. That's not me. I don't know no one by that name. Can I go now, nurse?'

125

'You can, Bailey. Take care.'

He closes the door carefully behind him and Sonny and I sit for a moment.

'Sylvie, may I say something?'

'Of course. I think I know – you're going to say he has scabies.'

'Yes, he does. I did notice that. We can get him a prescription, can't we?'

'Yes'

'No, it may be nothing, it's just – we had a lecture last week from GAV'

'GAV?'

'Growing Against Violence – it's a gang awareness raising movement. They go into schools and colleges, lecturing people about the rise of gang culture and how to detect involvement.'

'Gangs?'

'I think Bailey may be in a gang.'

'Isn't he rather young?'

'It all fits. Can I tell you about it?'

And over a new kind of bun that they have started serving fresh at the tea table outside her parents' Chinese restaurant, in Wardour Street, clever Sonny brings me up to speed about gang culture in Westminster. I am woefully out of date, it turns out. Social media has overturned old fashioned ways and the new breed of gangs spread toxic octopus' tentacles across postcodes, reaching far and wide.

'It's called Moon cake,' says Sonny.

'My mum says it's on the house, but just to warn you – it would be extremely bad etiquette to eat one all by yourself. No matter how small the Mooncake, we must share. Actually this one is quite big, isn't it?'

Sonny starts to cut the delicately layered cake carefully into small squares.

'Thanks so much, Sonny. What a treat.'

The sun has come out, shining on us through a gap where a building once was, that is now only girders preparing for a new-build onslaught.

' I prefer a decent croissant myself, but don't tell mum that. So… the gangs, it's extremely hierarchical'

'Tell me. I'm embarrassed that my gang knowledge is nil.'

'The man in overall charge is usually called "Top Boy", or something like that. He may be between twenty -two to twenty-five, sometimes older. Then he has a right hand man, with whom he will often share a genuine bond, though in the end the right hand man will need to take down the Top Boy, so it's never truly safe. Then there are the OGs or "olders" and the YGs, "youngers", or "youngies", who may be between thirteen and eighteen. And then you'll have the "tinys" or "babies".'

'Baby!'

'Exactly. The babies and tinys often have to copy the actions of their olders and youngers. Girls are at the absolute bottom of the hierarchy and usually have no status at all. They are property and disposable, even if they feel special for a short time.'

'Charming. What are the signs someone is in a gang?'

'Well, that's the thing – pretty much everything Bailey is exhibiting… reduced attendance, lateness, missed episodes he can't account for, withdrawal from trusted adults, pale and wan appearance. I didn't notice that he had any unexplained injuries – it might have been good to ask him, but I got the feeling you were taking it all gently, so as not to scare him off.'

'Yes, I got that feeling too. It hadn't been my intention, but the longer we were with him the more uncomfortably like a police interview I felt it was. I thought that might be his projection, I just had the sort of instinct to go gently with him. But maybe I should have been more directive. What do you think?'

Our competent students teach us so much. By asking them their views it not only empowers them to think as the professionals they are, but also genuinely helps us when we're at a loss. What's the point of unnecessary boundary drawing? Sonny is the 'expert' here, in the gang kingdom of the blind.

'Not sure. But they told us the gangs have strict rules, silence being perhaps the most potent. Also "earn and spend", because they can't store money for long, and a heavy shadow of violence, though not to uninvolved people. You don't score points for random attacks, in fact they can carry heavy penalties. Stabbing in the bum is common and stabbing in other discreet ways, like with knitting needles.'

'God.'

'I know. Oh and they make the kids store the drugs up their bottoms. Routinely. So there's sexual assault to consider, too.'

'He looked so frightened, don't you think? And closed.'

'Yes. And I was thinking – the way he disappeared for nine days, maybe he wasn't ill at home, but linked to county lines.'

'What's that, what's county lines?'

'County lines refers to the work that the gangs increasingly do outside their own patch and into towns in the provinces. Like the Woolwich gang famously link to East Anglia. And I heard that Central London links to the Midlands or, well anywhere there is a railway line.'

'Does the "line" refer to the railway line then?'

'To be honest, I'm not sure if it's that or the phone line. Phones, mobiles are incredibly important. Sacred, with the phone number of a Top Dog kept safe, often for years.'

'And they recruit the little ones, the "babies" to cross these lines?'

'Sometimes I think they use the older boys and "youngers" for that, but it was horrific what GAV told us… they send these kids out to somewhere like, say Norwich, tell them it's a nice "holiday in the country", then tie them into a drug den, where they basically keep them in squalor, as prisoners, their whole purpose being to sell drugs. They take over derelict properties – "abandos" they are sometimes called, but I think all the slang evolves and modifies quickly. They keep the boys high on Red Bull and, well probably a lot worse than that and then after nine days – that's the crucial date because at ten days it becomes illegal to be out of school – they send them home. Always with threats to keep silence, of course.'

'Nine days. Like Bailey.'

'I know.'

'He looked neglected too, didn't he?'

'Yes, and as though he hadn't seen much sun. I guess, with his mum not here to look after him he might have looked less loved anyway. I know its important not to jump to conclusions. And I don't think he was injured and he isn't wearing loads of layers. That's another sign – wearing layers of clothing because they don't want to get hurt, or so that they can shed them and change their appearance if people are after them.'

In my mind's eye I picture the genogram we had made together; Bailey with his mum circle 'RIP', his dad over in E Road, a vague and remote figure somehow, his brother…'.

'He was cagey about his brother, wasn't he?'

'Maybe an "older"?'

When we write case conference reports, we use a model where we are encouraged to sit with the unease of a family circumstance, consider the "grey areas". Family support in place for Bailey right now is a distinctly grey area.

'Right. Enough speculation. Straight to social services with all this, Sonny. It's been incredibly helpful having this conversation. Thank goodness for GAV. Thank heaven for you. I will call the social worker and Will Simpson, who was going to arrange an emergency professional meeting anyway. There are things we can do. I mean… there must be, mustn't there?'

Sonny looks doubtful and says uncertainly: 'Yes, although apparently they are notoriously hard to penetrate. The gangs tie families in; if Bailey's brother is involved to some degree, or even his father. It will be hard to prove anything and hard to keep Bailey safe. GAV told us that they even pay the electricity card for parents, or other household bills, to buy their silence.'

'And kids die. We know they do! That's not over dramatising, is it? I've worked with older children who have lost friends.'

'I know. Getting on for two hundred have died in the last decade.'

You know – I think Kayleigh and Ali have some clue.'

Sonny nods.

'I expect they do. Apparently, loads of the kids follow the traprat videos on social media. They knew his gang name, didn't they?'

'Yes. The name he denied all knowledge of, but with a certain bravado, I thought.'

'He gets kudos for that name. For being part of the gang. Other kids will be wary, but with an undisputed "respect", if you like. It's all about respect, though it's been proven that far from affording protection and social cohesion, the gang is actually one of the most precarious social groups to affiliate with. You are one hundred times more likely to be hurt if you're in a gang.'

'Kayleigh seemed more than generally interested in first aid for stabbing last week.'

'Oh dear. Oh yes and one more thing I remember – bereavement is meant to be the biggest risk factor. I suppose that fits with the Common Assessment Framework triangle – the falling away of a key protective factor. Oh, hello! Can I introduce you to my mum? Mum, this is Sylvie. I've told you about her.'

We shake hands and I enthuse to Sonny's mother about her wonderful daughter, of whom she must be so proud.

'She clever?'

'She is extremely clever. Yes, she is.'

Sonny blushes by the moon cake plates, pretending to sweep away crumbs.

'Mum, it's not all about that you know! Come on Sylvie, we need to go.'

We shake hands and bow and shake hands again and...

Yes, my own children, it really is that way. Sonny's mum likes to bow in greeting and she likes to ask me about her daughter's academic attainment. It may not be just racial stereotyping, after all, am I so very different about you? I love to hear when you are doing well.

But you don't 'bow in greeting'.

No, well maybe I'll start bowing.

'Sonny is a great asset to school nursing. And thank you again for the lovely…'.

Buns? You didn't say buns Mum?!

'Buns.'

Chapter Eleven

'Come in nurses, come in, lovely to see you all and thank you for coming. We're in the library today. I thought it might incline the girls to quietness and calm.'

'Thank you Alice. Wouldn't that be nice?'

'We can but hope. And this is their second and thankfully final **HPV** jab, isn't it? They should be used to the concept, though thinking back, is one ever? I never got used to needles. George, could you help the team with their clobber.'

An obliging caretaker helps us all up the polished oak stairs to the wooden paneled library, a legacy of the old school Langham Girls and maybe a canny move by Alice, who does know her girls so well. Usually we immunise them in a couple of adjacent empty, echoey classrooms, in an atmosphere that can get hot and hysterical, despite our best efforts.

Since we are so short staffed, school nurses from neighbouring boroughs have kindly (or in one case, grudgingly) offered to help out with our HPV sessions this term. Where we can, we return the favour and the days have a jolly, 'pulling-together- in-adversity feel. At Langham Girls I know we will be well cared for ourselves, with filter coffee and biscuits at break time. The girls have even been reasonably efficient at bringing their consent forms back, so we shouldn't have to call too many parents mid-session, and as Alice pointed out, it is their second jab, so maybe they are used to all the fuss now and the library will cast a magical calm to proceedings.

We set about transforming the elegant room into a miniature field hospital, complete with makeshift 'casualty area' for fainters.

'I've read that one in a hundred people is likely to pass out, when being given an injection,' I hear Sonny telling Alan, a hint of anxiety in her tone. We seem to have adopted Sonny, at this stage in the term, her own practice teacher in South London having gone on 'long term sick'. Long term sick is becoming endemic in community nursing. Not that we are complaining at having Sonny around. I think she is an undisputed asset. It's hard to tell quite what Alan thinks.

'Are you both happy to immunise, Sonny and Alan? As supernumerary, you are not obliged to of course, but as you have signed all the relevant paperwork and have been assessed, you are qualified and safe to, if you want the practice'

'Yes, fine Sylvie,' says Alan briskly, setting out his wares on a blue clinical towel covered table.

'Cotton wool balls, pen, plasters… Sonny, could you tape these bin liners to the side of my table? One yellow, one black. Thanks.'

'Yes, sure, of course, Alan. Um, I'm not so incredibly keen, Sylvie. That is, I am of course fine to immunise and if you need me to I will, but there seem to be quite a few of you… might I help in other ways?'

Alan registers nothing, but sends off almost visible waves of boundless joy.

'There's always plenty to do, Sonny.' I say.

'And when we get a quiet moment, we can give you a little practice on a straightforward person. Alan is excellent with the needle-shy girls.'

'Is everyone else okay? Settling in?'

134

I look around at the long suffering team, who have been prepared to turn up in all weathers, to all kinds of school sites, where a cuppa and a bun is a bonus and by no means guaranteed, but what will be guaranteed is three hours of intense injecting against the school clock, as we try our hardest to make every interaction personal and discreet, as though the children were in the comfort of their own GP surgery.

Sonny is taping bags to the side of every immunisers table now;

'There is strong evidence that immunising in school increased uptake and helps meet the target of herd immunity.'

'Ha! Herd's the right word for this lot, isn't that right guys? Noisy rabble!'

I don't like this one much. I am always glad she works for another borough most of the time, but we have to have her help today. We always end up roping her in to sessions, because we are so short staffed. And she knows it. Privately, I think of her as not one of us.

You 'other' her.

Is that what I do, Theo?

Just saying…

'They're not a rabble' I say to her.

She folds her arms and chuckles infuriatingly. As I'm about to open my mouth to utter something even more prickly and inane, there is a deafening sound of feet and screeching on the stairs. Philomena appears, grinning at the library door.

'Hello Sylvie and the gang. I've been asked to supervise . This is 8B, are you ready for 'em? Hope someone faints. Or has a heart attack.'

The HPV jab or human papillomavirus vaccine, was introduced in 2008, to protect girls from the virus that causes cancer of the cervix. It is given to girls of around thirteen because this is the time it is thought their cells are most receptive. It is potentially life-saving and is not an encouragement to promiscuity, but there has been and continues to be resistance, more from some parents than from children themselves.

New vaccines always cause jitters and the cause for HPV was not helped by the death up North somewhere, of an unfortunate girl by a completely unrelated, hitherto undetected heart condition hours after her first jab, soon after the introduction of the vaccine. This has gone down nationwide in the annals of history, and the tabloids had had a field day.

'My dad says it's not safe, Miss.'

'Remember the girl who died?'

'My mum thinks it's a conspiracy by the government to make you have it.'

'Someone told me it gives you Aids.'

We always give some health promotion to dispel these myths and answer valid queries, starting as soon into the academic year as we can, reminding them at appropriate moments, but the vaccine is still less than a decade old and there will be worries.

'At least it's only two jabs now, my sister had three in her year.'

'Is two enough, nurse? I don't want to die of cancer!'

They pronounce it 'cansaaar'.

In most NHS Trusts, school nursing teams were tasked with delivering the vaccines, as we tend to be, for most immunisations of school aged children. Sonny is right and herd immunity needs to be 80% for the vaccine to be effective population-wide. And schools are evidenced as the best places to access the 'hard to reach' population. All such good reasons to be here today, ticking off an entirely measurable and quantifiable public health intervention. A 'quick win', if you like.

'But I hate imms sessions, if I'm truly honest,' I mutter to Ricci, who has come by with Nelly, en route to a New Birth Visit.

'It all looks pretty ship shape, Sylvie. Relatively calm and look... there is the lovely Philomena tending to the ailing ones. Wishing drama on them, so she can practice her first aid.'

'Oh it's fine, but there is always the worry that it might not be.'

'You've got adrenaline drawn up on every table, haven't you?'

'Yes, of course, and the nurses will all be just fine. We have paramedic Philomena, after all. But I wouldn't be sorry if I never had to run another session. There's the palaver of keeping the cold chain, lugging those bulky boxes in and out of the taxi - which is invariably late arriving - making us late to our schools, so we are wrong footed from the start. And we get unceremoniously dumped on the pavement in the middle of London streets with these cumbersome cool bags, shopping trolleys, syringes and all. We are a walking hazard.'

'You love it, Sylvie. Moan over?'

'Yes. Sorry.'

'Hey - none of these girls has had breakfast, Sylvie. Didn't you tell them 'its important?'

'Oh God, her!' Ricci ducks behind the cool bags. 'I was hoping she'd retired, or died. Still going strong then?'

'Aha! You were trying to offer her to me as a sop at the beginning of term. Your true feelings are revealed. Of course I've told the girls about breakfast. I loathe her, Ricci. So do the girls! Look, hardly anyone is going to her for their vaccine.'

But I'm laughing, because it is funny how collectively we all grumble about 'her' when we couldn't do without her and what I've said isn't true at all, because she's actually quite nice to the girls. It's we who struggle with her.

'Hate, hate, hate, ah the true spirit of community nursing lives on. Compassion in care embodied. There's always one, isn't there? I'm going to miss all the internal politics when I retire. I'd better be off, but I had a message for you; Bailey Bennet's social worker rang and there's to be an emergency professionals' meeting this afternoon. Will you be done here or do you need me to stand in? Poor little chap…'

'No, we're fine. That's good about Bailey. Thanks Ricci. We are getting through the girls pretty smoothly, despite her. I'm sure we will be done by lunch time. I will take Sonny to the professionals meeting. She's a fount of knowledge about gangs, you know.'

'Who would have thought it, to look at her. I'm on my way then. Have a good morning ladies, Alan, Olly dear. Keep up the good work and all that. Come on Nell.'

'Skiver! You health visitors don't know you're born!'

Ricci ignores her. Nelly manages a loyal little growl as she and her master skip off down the oaken stairs.

The emergency meeting for Bailey takes place at one of our social services buildings, in the centre of town, a quick tube ride from the school. Our immunisation session has passed remarkably without incident, to Philomena's disappointment and profitably for Sonny, who was able to 'practice' on a few unwitting scholars at the end, when there was less noise and haste. She is now glowing with the confidence of one who has mastered a practical skill. Giving injections was almost the first technical skill we learnt when I was a student nurse. As legend has it we practiced on oranges, but mainly we practiced on people, with the beady eye of a ward sister to spur us on. I was a bit hit and miss in the early days, but the trick is to give an intramuscular jab firmly and fast. Over in the blink of an eye works for the majority and keeps the queue down, hysteria to a minimum. If you're lucky you get a gratifyingly incredulous 'Is that it? I never even felt nothing. Oh, my days! It doesn't hurt at all, I swear!'

138

And some of the children need endless care and lots of time, because people have very good reasons for being scared of needles and sometimes no tangible reason at all, but the fear is still real. We pride ourselves on taking that time, helping the children through so that their next experience is less to be dreaded.

'You still give it that swiftly, though, Alan. Even when they're scared?'

Sonny is perched up next to Alan on a little stool, watching his every move.

'Yes. Lots of time with them, as long as they need, with no sense of rush, but when you give it, do it fast and firm and have the cotton wool ready to press on immediately after so they see no blood. Don't forget to tell them not to move their arm before, though. That is important, so you don't scratch them.'

'Or yourself, young man. You don't want a needle-stick injury to add to your woes!'

I wish I could have shut her up, calling out across the library with her patronizing, doom laden warnings. But she was right with her needle-stick warning too, I have to concede. And over break time, when most of us were grabbing the fifteen minutes' respite to dive into the biscuit barrel, she spent time talking gently and sensitively to a girl who had a history of self-harm and felt self-conscious about revealing her arm.

Sonny learnt a lot this morning. Her head is so full of academic excellence, but they don't always get the time for developing practical skills that we did. Nursing is holding many things in the balance.

Hello you, sorry to disturb your busy school nursing morning, but AMAZING news.

Finn, what?

I have an idea, but want to see it written

The town committees have said yes! Suddenly and without warning, to

139

all our plans. I love them! We are good to go! North Wind Pavilion Community Arts Café here we come! We need a better name.

YAY! AMAZING'!

Yes. Must go. Can't wait to see you at half term. Bring your paint brush. Oh and there's a secret even better bit.

Tell.

It's a show not tell, Sylvie. See you soon.

***

Now we are gathered round a huge board table; representatives from school, social services, the gang prevention team, Bailey's GP, the bereavement counsellor he has always effectively eluded, and the police. How many agencies does it take to make one little boy safe?

'Thank you all for coming at such short notice. Please feel free to eat your lunch. I did invite Mr Bennett, but he declined to attend and Bailey's older brother is not contactable at the moment. Now, if we could all introduce ourselves…'.

Two hours on and an interim plan to safeguard Bailey has been made. We have shared our information, in the light of which it's agreed that Bailey is significantly at risk. Sonny has contributed assertively. My pride in her momentarily eclipses my worry for Bailey. But looking at the Common Assessment Framework triangle, which she has so conscientiously brought with her for reference, it is plain as day that Bailey's wellbeing is compromised on every level. Child development needs, parenting capacity and family and environmental factors are all in question. Bailey is not safe in his life at the moment. He has also been identified in a 'traprat' video and has been spotted on CCTV, hanging round Camden Bridge.

'Of course, in Central London these kids are particularly vulnerable because it's an international hub for crime, not just local.' Says the conference Chair

'And our information suggests that it's likely both his older brother and his father are not uninvolved. Hence their silence and general lack of cooperation.'

School nurses, like social workers and teachers, work alongside parents. It goes against the grain to suspect the worst of those who should be caring, but numerous serious case reviews teach us that we must hold all possibilities in the balance. Lord Laming and Eileen Munro have been particularly vociferous on this subject in their safeguarding reports.

This plan will include a child protection medical, lots more talking to Bailey and interim foster care - and the only certainty is that this will be the first of many meetings.

And hovering mindfully for a moment?

Oh, Theo. I just want to take Bailey home.

And you can't, but hold that feeling in mind and acknowledge it for what it is.

I want to take them all home.

The Chair thanks us for our attendance and calls the meeting to close. If he wasn't before, little Bailey is now firmly in 'the system'.

Sonny and I walk back to Soho Square subdued.

'Do you think we have helped Bailey today? Made his life better, or easier, Sylvie?

We have reached the green tiled, three arched hall we call home.

'It's always warm in here, isn't it? I like the atmosphere,' says Sonny.

I shake my head, because that is one of the big questions; how much do we help when we 'escalate concerns', alert the authorities, follow procedure? Quite often we make it worse.

'I don't know, Sonny. But we don't have a choice with safeguarding. It is always a bit clunky. And maybe we can stay alongside Bailey, through school. Try and be there for him, as objective, neutral support.'

I'm also wondering about the country boarding school and whether it might be possible to lift Bailey right out of his Soho world and replant him in a safe haven far away. Might that work? It doesn't always, but maybe this is the legacy his mother has left him, her conscientious preparations for his secondary school which were not even alluded to in our emergency meeting. I make a note to talk to Will Simpson.

And to Sonny's smaller question: 'Yes, I always find this hall warm. And feel it welcomes me home. But some people find it cold and spooky.'

'Do they? How interesting. My mum says that buildings have as much personality as people and that we respond to them in accordance with our own spirit.'

'Old Chinese proverb?'

Sonny grins.

'Something like that.'

Chapter Twelve

Every term sweeps us into its rushing river. With no time to draw breath we are swept along on the tide of events and then beached abruptly on the shore for an enforced half term break. It is hard to relax and unwind to order, so we get ill instead, spending the first few days of our week moping round with colds and sore throats.

Your Threat and Drive systems are on overdrive, taking all your energy. Come back to your Soothing system of emotional regulation.

Thanks Theo, but how?

Trust the Soothing system, your higher brain. It is there all the time, it hasn't gone away.

I think it alludes me...

Collaboration, community, safety, boundless love. All there. Return to them.

Right. Easy peesy.

We have packed our late-teen children into the car and brought them away from London to unwind in Cromer and hopefully feel able to revise a little.

'When are we old enough to be left in London, Mum?'

'Not quite yet, I'm thinking.'

'Cromer feels like home.'

'London feels like fun.'

'Dad can never quite relax in London, living "above the shop".

'I wish we did live above a shop.'

'Or a cinema.'

'What's on at Cromer cinema?'

Relentless Whitsun rain drives against the windows of the never salubrious, but for us, compelling pier cafe. As well as the inevitable illness for summer half term, there is the equally inevitable shit weather. It's almost comforting in its terribleness. There is nothing to be done but stay in, or walk in wellies along a wet beach. The children decamp to the cinema and at last Finn and I have time, actual real time to spend together.

'It occurs to me that you will still need the Pier cafe to escape from your own café enterprise.'

Finn grimaces and (not 'but') her eyes are bright with the happiness of hope realised.

'I know. Be careful what you wish for and all that. The café vision coming to life is astonishing. Huge shifts have been made in the community, the goodwill, kindness and creativity out there is boundless, a joy to harness, but you and I will probably still sneak off here, where a cappuccino means boiled milk with a bit of instant coffee sprinkled on the top. Good old Norfolk "cup of chino".'

'That "boundless" word you mention, Finn. Collaboration, community, and boundless love.'

'What?'

'Something Theo said, you know, the guy we go to talk to at work.'

'Oh yes, aka God"

'Ricci's image of God, maybe?'

'Boundless love sounds like the sort of thing God might advocate.'

'True.'

We watch the rain on the pane and the grey sea beyond. A Norfolk sea might be ocean blue, but there are many grey, flat days too, to lose oneself in. I love these days. Is this what Theo means? I will visualize this comforting, containing place next time my soothing system gets out of synch by drive and threat.

After a nice pause for watching raindrops, Finn asks: 'Are you okay, Sylvie?'

'I think so.'

'Writing it all down, the children and their different worlds, their complex lives, your feelings about school nursing, your passion for it all...'.

'I hate the word passion.' I snap.

'Oh, sorry.'

'No, I'm sorry, but I mean I've noticed it is a word The Powers use when they want to shelve their own responsibility for cutting services, making the National Health Service a little bit worse every day. When we rail against the cuts and the changes and the task driven, empathy-lacking processes, when we point out that the child's voice is being lost, they will say patronizingly; "oh, but you're so passionate about school nursing", then they can dismiss it and us. For "passionate" read "naive, blinded by love, impractical and immature".'

'Yes, I get that,' Finn says, quietly.

'And writing about it at the same time as living it has done what Theo tries to get us to do, I suppose... what we should all perhaps do in our lived worlds, if we can. It has helped me step outside of my immediate thoughts as they roll along and reflect on them a bit. Does that make sense?'

'Yes.'

'Because it's a mad world, Finn. Trying to do a tiny bit of school nursing, when there are so few of us. The other day at Drop-in, Phil was sitting in, eating her lunch, when three younger girls were talking openly about the pressures that have led them to self-harm. They went into detail about how they do it and what they've done. These three are "known self-harmers" – how awful to speak as casually as that, but we do, to mean they have been referred to CAMHS and are being supported, I hope. But "it's not just us", they'd said. "Loads of our friends feel anxious and stressed and try harming themselves. Loads of us have panic attacks."

I had brought my bubbles out, to show them a quick trick that can help steady breathing – you know, blowing through the bubbles wand and watching the bubbles? So we had done that for a bit, and we looked at the bubbles floating around and bursting gently around us. And I told them that Alice, that's their head teacher, you know, was developing a whole school approach to tackling such issues, that people were listening, that we were seeking expert advice…

'Arty Slimreed?'

'Yes, she and the mental health charity she works with are great and have lots of sound ideas for working in schools, relating uncomfortable ideas to parents and carers, helping us all learn more about why people turn to hurting themselves to give themselves some release, some control over uncertainty and frightening feelings. But at the end of the lunch hour, when they had all gone off to lessons, Philomena shook her head and said; "I dunno about Drop-in, Sylvie. It's more like drop in the ocean, innit?" and she's right.

146

'She's so clever. And funny.'

'Isn't she? Wonderful girl. But she's right too. It is just a drop in the ocean, all the public health initiatives are. I think we are floundering.'

I'd wanted to hear from Finn about her pastel painted tables and her bunting, every last detail of the incongruous group of volunteers who were daily proffering their time, talent and goodwill to her creative enterprise as it gathered shape. Beginnings, new ideas, collaboration and community. Instead, I was taking our precious time being sad. Stupid. Change the subject.

'I wanted to ask you about buns, Finn. The children say, well Ricci and everyone really says I call everything a bun, but what really is the definition of a bun?'

Finn puts her hand lightly over mine.

'We can talk about buns, of course and my plans - there is something else by the way, a surprise I haven't even showed you yet - but it is okay to be sad for a while and not even talk about anything.'

So we look out to sea together, contemplating a London world that doesn't seem so far away today. We are present in a moment where Soho, Cromer and all our worlds can be held, past, future and now.

And then we agree that warm milk with instant coffee stirred in is surprisingly nice and would go well with a small bun.

***

The sun has come by mid-week. My children and Finn's have come out with the sun and other half-terming teens to offer their services to Finn's café committee. There is sanding down and painting up, there are walls to wash down and beds to weed. There is crockery to wash and stack and the first trial cakes to bake in a magnificent and absurdly expensive-looking sky blue Aga that has been generously donated and fitted by the new owners of a nearby stately home.

'What a beautiful thing.'

'Uplifting to behold, isn't it? The same colour as your girls' school's uniform. And it fits just perfectly into the kitchen space, which is bigger than it looks, thus solving all our heating as well as cooking issues, for bleaker days, when we need it to be snug here inside.'

'How incredibly kind.'

'I know. It wasn't quite the right colour for their new kitchen, so rather than send it back, they passed it on to us and paid for the specialist Aga fitter. People are giving so much. But even your babes and mine wielding a paintbrush for an hour away from their revision makes a big difference.'

'I think mine are only too glad of a distraction.'

'Yes. And by the way, I checked with my chief baking volunteer and have a definition for you.'

Finn rummages in the pocket of her dungarees, pulling out a Post It note.

'A bun is a small, sometimes sweet, bread or bread roll. Though they come in many shapes or sizes they are most commonly hand-sized or smaller, with a round top and flat bottom. Buns are usually made from flour, sugar, milk, yeast and butter. Does that help?'

She hands it to me;

'Hugely. Thanks. So, a slice of Victoria sponge…'.

'Is definitely not a bun, no.'

'But it's made with flour, sugar and butter…'

'But not yeast. Small with round top and flat bottom, that's the rule.'

'Right. Although there are quite a few qualifiers there, aren't there? "Usually made with", "*Commonly* made from…".

'I suppose you could go on calling everything a bun, if it's one change too many, Sylvie.'

'I think I may.'

'Now, come on, I have the surprise to show you.

Before Finn's community initiative, the cafe had been a derelict old pavilion, standing out against the windy old weather for over a century, just on the corner of Cromer where the poppy fields meet the lighthouse path.

'The stairs are still rickety, the men are working on them next week and until then it's just by special permission, but they've made good the floor. Follow me up, but mind your footing.'

'What was the building originally used for?'

'I think it's been many things. There was a vast hotel behind here, built in the early Victorian era, when Cromer became for a short time, a fashionable seaside resort. They pulled the hotel down in the 1940s, but left the pavilion standing. The council wrangle went on for so long because it is a listed building and you can see why, but no one was caring for it and the floorboards up here on this floor were rotten. You can see how much they've done, look!'

'Oh!'

'Oh Sylvie, don't lean on that banister, not quite there yet, but what do you think?'

She has led me into a space that is all light and simple lines. Lime washed floorboards, chalk painted woodwork and floor length shutter windows thrown open onto a long pavilion balcony.

'Okay to walk on the floor now, even out here?'

'Yes, yes, completely fine. Look at the view!'

We move across the room and out to lean on the balcony railing. Boundless sea.

'It's...'

'I know. When we were first thinking about the café, I hadn't really considered this upstairs area. It had been out of bounds for so long, that we had ruled it out, mentally. But when the café plans got going and people took my original ideal and ran with it, like a kite that's really going to fly, I realized that I would need another kind of space as well. Somewhere to paint, somewhere separate from the community bustle below. I remembered the upstairs, stole up one evening with Ben and, well, fell in love with up here too.'

'This room is the real gem of the Norfolk coast.'

'Isn't it?'

'Like a kind of giant, empty beach hut, all ready for your ideas.'

'And yours, and others. My plan is to make it make it a communal space for writing or painting, with a space or desk for each person, coffee – yes, and buns from below for sustenance and the company of others so we don't feel alone, when we are trying to do our own creating things. Convivial, you know? But quiet. Oh, and sometimes, to raise more monies, we could have concerts up here, or band nights maybe. It's pretty big, you know?'

'I can see. It's...'

But I am speechless for what it is, because it is so completely what Finn needed that there are no more words to say. It is proof that dreams can be realised, that's what it is.

'But Finn, promise me you will keep some of this space just for you? Remember what you wanted at the beginning – to facilitate a place for others to get together and collaborate and be communal, but also a space for you?'

Finn scrapes at a window frame, where some putty has been left.

'I know. Don't worry, I have remembered that bit. When all the grants were sorted and the monies tied up and the council happy, I built into the contract two hours every morning that are free just for me; six until eight every morning. You know I'm an early riser and done-up by mid-morning. But the early part of the day is when I'm at my best and the beauty of that is that the café will not even open until 9.00am. I can come earlier than 6.00am if I want, if Ben doesn't mind.'

'The twins are way old enough to sort themselves out for breakfast and getting off to school, aren't they?'

'Completely. They never eat breakfast anyway. Do yours? Do any kids? And they go to Uni in September, anyway. Empty nest, Sylvie. Need to guard against that.'

'It's...'.

I still can't form an articulate description of what it is, this oasis, this sanctuary, this soothing system for my friend Finn.

'I knew you'd understand, Sylvie. And the best thing is you haven't asked me what I am going to paint.'

'Why would I do that?'

'It's what everyone else seems to do. As if they doubt my ability to have a creative thought in my head, without a practical little plan.'

'It's not really about "what", is it? More about getting the space and then seeing what comes out.'

'Exactly. And if that's nothing and I just sit here looking at the sea…'

'Then you'll be being "mindful", in the modern way!'

'So I will.'

Chapter Thirteen

At the end of half term the pull to stay in our Cromer lives had been strong.

'Oh, there'll be plenty of time for hanging about together when we've all got old and retired, Sylvie. Both the hubbies in their sheds, or crab fishing together. Us two painting and writing away, long after ability and sight desert us. Back to work with you both for now,' said Finn.

'Not long until the summer holidays anyway. And we've reserved your writing space in the studio. That's the main thing.'

'Whenever I need space in my head, I will think of your empty room, looking out over the poppies and towards the sea. Bring Cromer to Soho. Crocus would have approved of the studio, wouldn't she?'

'Crocus Lettison. Was that really her name? That school! We never flourished there. If it hadn't been for Crocus, pottering about in her smock, in that bulb nurturing way... She was a good artist, though. Slade school trained. She taught us shading.'

And as always, it is proving hard to remember Finn's studio by the sea now we are back in the Big Smoke. Even our own solid, shabby old house fades in my mind's eye, when I'm back into rushing river and heading downstream.

***

'Upstream thinking.' Daphne extols the students, as they meet for almost their last session of the academic year, before they move into their month of consolidated practice with their respective teams. We have been invited along too, to mark this momentous stage of the year.

'One of the founding principles of good public health practice - and still as fresh an image today as when coined by John McKinley in 1974 at the Ottowa Convention. Someone remind me what it means to us? No, someone other than Sonny. Alan dear?'

I notice Alan and Sonny are sitting together.

'It means looking upstream to see why the people are falling in, rather than pulling out the bodies at the bottom. It's a metaphor.'

'It is, it is, well done Alan, a metaphor, albeit a rather obvious one, for our own practice. Prevention is best and failing that…?'

'Early intervention,' they chorus.

This band of health visitor and school nurse students have now been well trained in public health principles. Shame these committed students are being launched, with their high ideals, into a climate where the reverse is so often practised. Where investment in all our preventative services is being cut, cut, cut and where it is, apparently, the responsibility of the individual to pull themselves out of the stream, however strong the current. I keep my despondent thoughts to myself, because I am tired of them too. I want to be hopeful, see promise and opportunity even when the light seems dim. Daphne and Chloe move on to the socio-economics of health and the inequality agenda. Again, much rehearsed and lessons well learnt. The students won't forget abiding principles learnt here. They will help shape the public health of the next generation.

Daphne holds up a cuddly toothy rodent who wears a mauve bonnet and ribbon. The students laugh, all her darlings now, transgressions forgotten or forgiven at this stage in the year;

'And who is this, students?'

'Michael the Marmot.'

'Yes! Lovely Professor Sir Michael, who I keep by my pillow, such is my commitment to the cause. Marmot wrote his governmental review on inequality, the book *Status Syndrome* and most recently he wrote… okay, Sonny, if no one else remembers?'

'Mind The Gap.'

'Yes, yes, thank you Sonny dear. Remember Marmot and Munroe and Laming, too. Lord Laming is coming to prominence again this week with his latest report on Looked After Children. Remember what you have learnt already and keep abreast of current policy by reading every nursing journal you can lay your hands on. Don't become complacent, because the waters move fast in public health practice. Chloe, have you anything to add, as a final *bon mot* for the students and their long suffering practice teachers gathered here today? Anything that leaps to mind?'

Chloe is usually content to let Daphne take centre stage when the space becomes more theatre than lecture.

'Non, non, mais…. one small thought, peut-etre; in all the talk of populations, profiling communities and such, please do not overlook the individual. You are nurses and you do not cease to be nurses. Infirmieres. I do not mean that the social model of health should not apply. The individual needs to be considered within this model, naturellement. But never forget to treat each person as the unique individual that they are, n'est-ce pas?'

Chloe surveys us calmly, Daphne clutches Michael the Marmot to her breast.

'C'est tout. Et bonne chance, tout le monde. Bonne chance.'

***

Endings begin early into this half of term. The Year Elevens have already 'left' school, to come back almost as visitors for their exams, their places in the sixth form dependent on appropriate grades. It can be a strangely disconnected time. Finn and I had reminisced about our own dim, distant experiences, over half term;

'We were dismissed before the start of our exams, do you remember that time? Long study days, too much freedom all of a sudden, unless one was very organised, mature and understood how to work. Were you, Finn?'

'God no! I just drifted in and out of the garden, pulled out by the sun and my need to get brown legs, then in again by the obligation to study, without any real idea of what independent study is. My parents got on my nerves. I felt quite lonely, actually, thinking back.'

'Me too and I think that's the experience of lots of children now, ours too, probably. Parents don't stop being busy with their own lives, home can be unnervingly quiet in the day. A lot of our young people in Westminster go to the library to work. Even if they get less done, they have each other.'

'But it was better when we actually started the exams, wasn't it?'

'Kind of. Although I remember one English exam where I'd come in, having not really connected with any teachers or friends for a while, and I just felt the exam slipping away from me. It was a subject I was even okay at. I still have nightmares about that. Writing one or two nonsensical sentences, then watching the clock in a kind of frozen panic.'

156

'Did you say anything afterwards?'

'There wasn't really anyone to speak to. I didn't know the teachers who were adjudicating and I felt so disconnected, I just slipped away. I remember walking through Norwich to catch the train home and feeling separate from everyone and everything. It would have been useful to talk to someone then, although I wouldn't have known where to start.'

'Lovely as our parents were, they were – just as you say – busy with their own lives and it wasn't the thing to confide in teaching staff then, was it?'

'No. I felt guilty and stupid, so I just blotted it out and batted on. Like we did.'

'Boarding schools can be better at that stage, I think, maybe? Some kids go home, but there is often the option to hang around, do your revision and temper it with some fun and a bit of sports, you know?'

'I know, but I guess even if it were free, boarding wouldn't work for everyone. People have so many legitimate reservations. 'You don't have kids to send them away' and all that. I will never be sure what I think. Every child is an individual, I suppose. No system is perfect and other such clichés.'

Bailey's social worker has invited me to visit a boarding school with her and Bailey. Following the strategy meeting, Will Simpson and I had mentioned Bailey's mother's forward thinking in entering Bailey for the entrance exam for the boarding school. This had been followed up and it seemed, for him, that it might be a feasible reality. They would need to fix up a consistent foster care placement for him in the holidays, but for once social services had move swiftly on this. More investigation of these suspicious nine days absent from school, by talking to Bailey and a child protection medical had revealed that he had indeed been sent away, by a gang to an 'abando' far out of

London. Bailey is now having frequent one to one therapeutic time with a specialist psychologist and has been found a caring foster placement locally.

'Actually caring?' I express my doubts to Will Simpson

'Yes, very much so.' says Will.

'He is with a solid couple who live nearby and have cared for children who have complex situations before. Nothing quite like this, though. Poor Bailey. I had no idea about the level of gang crime impacting on this age group, before this all came out. We have GAV coming in to talk to all the head teachers at our next forum and we are working closely with police and social services now. Because it is not just Bailey, is it? Bailey is the boy we know about and can now help. It's the others out there.'

'Not everyone is as exquisitely vulnerable as Bailey became, I suppose, but yes. It is all out there and we don't know enough.'

I feel deeply proud of Sonny for raising our awareness, for quite possibly saving Bailey. Public health Chloe's way, one person at a time.

Will tells me: 'I'm pleased you're going down with Bailey to the boarding school. That's a school we have a long association with, one of the old time charity schools that still retains its links with London. I have seen them transform a receptive child and it will ensure there's a distance between Bailey and the influences.'

'I'm looking forward to it. I'm surprised and touched he wanted me to go with him.'

'He likes you, I think. Says you're funny. Well you are quite comical, aren't you?'

'Am I?'

'The children say you're funny in their sex ed classes.'

'Good comic material.'

'Quite. Bailey is beginning to get his sense of humour back and he is naturally sociable. He is very enthusiastic about the school too. His mother taught him that education is the way "out", but he had lost his way after she died. It's not for everyone, boarding and being removed from your home environment, but it might be just the thing for Bailey.'

Bailey, his social worker, his foster mum and I meet at Victoria Station. Bailey is grinning on the platform, sipping a large banana milkshake through a straw.

'It's like Harry Potter school, Sylvie. It has its own station!'

'Amazing.'

'And it's called a hospital, but that's just an old name for school.'

This school had been founded in the City of London, in Elizabethan times, for the 'poor of London' and had judiciously moved out to West Sussex in Victorian times, when land and labour were relatively cheap. Now, it offers an alternative choice of education for children 'from all walks of life'. The common denominator is that they need to be academically able, which of course raises its own questions around inequality, as some have such a head start up the 'Marmot' mountain. The queue for the entrance exam, I remembered from delivering another child there one March day, was also quite like auditions for Harry Potter, with a queue stretching round the block of the Fulham Primary school they had taken over for the purpose. Places are hugely in demand, but there is a priority given to children with a social need. Bailey has already passed the exam and his need is undisputed.

'You look well, Bailey.'

'Yeah. I've been through some shit, but things are looking up, Sylvie. You heard about this school?'

'Kind of, but I've never been. Thanks for asking me along.'

'It was Peace's idea to ask you. Peace – meet Sylvie. Peace and Percy is looking after me until they find me a permanent, but I'm hoping that the permanent will be Peace and Percy, cos they're nice.'

Peace and I shake hands, Bailey beams. The social worker suggests we all hop on the train, so it doesn't leave without us.

Bailey seems like a younger boy again. His burden is falling away from him and he is relying on adults to care for him a bit. There is so much to unpack. It is never a simple happy ending, but Bailey has a clear sense of what is right for him and some of the natural order has been restored.

We spend a happy hour travelling down to Horsham and the one stop beyond. We alight from the train at a country station, all cow parsley and gentle pasture. In the distance, we can see a tall red brick water tower. I think it looks quite daunting, but Bailey has his eyes on the horizon.

'There it is. That's my school. Come on!'

And we set off, up the path and over the open fields, to the school, Bailey leading the way.

***

Back in the very centre of town later, I learn that First Aid is taking on a life of its own. Mobile ambulance workers, based in the walk-in centre that occupies the ground floor of our building, beyond the graciously haunted hall, have noticed our antics and seem not unimpressed.

Ricci is having a chat with one, perched on the wall outside the building, catching the evening sun, when I arrive back from my day out with Bailey. I have notes to drop off. Nelly, nosing round the lamp posts on her long lead, barks a greeting.

'Oh, how did it go in the countryside, Sylvie? How is the dear boy? Sylvie – this is Tony, who has a suggestion for our First Aiders.'

'Hello Tony good to meet you.' Tony has parked his ambulance bike and is wearing the full regalia of a paramedic.

Tony shakes my hand, a strong, decisive grip.

Pleased to meet you. I was saying to Ricci - those kids have a better grasp of the basics than many of our staff. They could be cadets, if any of them are interested? I'm setting up a group in September. Not to diminish the work you've been doing with them, but I understand from Ricci that the sessions will round up after this term? Some of them might like to join cadets and put their training onto a more formal footing? Keeps them off the streets, too.'

I like Tony's plan. The Powers haven't visited yet, but the threat of change hovers. Ricci, Alan, Sonny and I have loved the unique way this little group has evolved, but know it is not sustainable in the longer term. The children's individual circumstances will naturally change after the summer holiday and more significantly, we don't even know if we will still have a school health service based here in the heart of town.

'There are moves to redistribute us, Tony. The rent's expensive for an ever diminishing space and the Trust now feels it would be cheaper for them to house us elsewhere in the borough.'

Tony shakes his head.

'But your families and schools are here!'

'And arguably, we can hop on a bus to reach them, like everyone else does these days. You can see their point.'

'Suppose. But it's a great building, isn't it? Don't you just love this main hall?' Tony gesticulates to the front door. 'Echoes of the past in there.

Sometimes when I'm clearing up my stuff after everyone's gone home it feels... oh never mind.'

'Well anyway, we're having a final session in a couple of weeks; might you come along and suggest the cadets plan? I mean, even if we do start up again after the summer holidays, we rely on the good weather, so our little group is specifically seasonal.'

'Sure. I'd love to.'

'And in the meantime, can we borrow your practice defibrillator machine?'

We watch Tony mount the impressively kitted out ambulance bike and wobble off round the square.

'So, how was the school? Don't get me wrong, I'm not for sending every kid away to school, but that boy so deserves a break.'

'Ricci, it was wonderful....!'

I launch into a fulsome description of the unusual school, with its uniform of navy blue coats, breeches and yellow socks dating back to Tudor time, the brass band which marches them all into lunch every day, the complete mixture of kids which give you the surreal impression that you're in one of our local playgrounds, but all replanted down there in the country, with proper space for games and libraries for learning...

'And Bailey liked it?'

'That was the strangest thing, really. Bailey fitted in like a duck to water, the second he arrived. I think it helped that it had been something he'd talked through with his mum. He feels a link with her because of it. He feels proud that she sought out the school and made an effort, her last and almighty effort as it transpired, on his behalf. But it all suited him, he just seemed at home.'

'That uniform sounds bizarre.'

'I know, but apparently the children voted to keep it, when they had the choice. The boy who showed us round – he also went to Piccadilly Primary, so that was good and Bailey remembered him – but he said that the uniform is a good leveler. He said people come from rough estates and pay no fees, or they come from posh homes and pay full fees and lots of range in between, but once you get down here and everyone's wearing the completely *mental* uniform, everyone looks the same.'

'The guy has a point, I guess.'

'Yes. He also said that lots of them have parents who have died, or other adverse circumstances, which makes it a bit weird, perhaps, having them all down there together, but the pastoral care is meant to be second to none. Bailey was not even trying to play it cool on the way home. He was on cloud nine, bouncing on the seat. And his foster carers are great, by the way.'

'Let's just hope they can keep him safe through the summer, then. School worlds are as different as every family are, one from another, aren't they?'

I'm noticing that Ricci has become deeply involved in our school nursing cases this term.

'How was First Aid? I am sorry I had to miss it. Thanks so much for taking it on.'

'Oh, it was fine. They are just adorable, everyone. Lots of goss, just where to start...'.

We move into our haunted hall and sit together on the Arts and Crafts stair, for Ricci to bring me up to speed, while Nelly waits patiently. Everything seems to have happened and I feel I have been away months, not just a day. According to Ricci, Kayleigh has had her plaits cut off; Ana has unceremoniously dumped her chef boy because she found out he had several girlfriends; Mrs Oppah has applied to do her nursing training, Plank and his family have a three bedroomed flat confirmed in Barking and are moving out of the hostel at the end of the month; and Ali is out of his plaster and keeps falling over because he is not yet used to his own weight.

'So much news!'

'I know. And did you realise, no you probably didn't because you are not an observant person, Sylvie – Alan and Sonny are an item?'

'No?!'

'Yep. Planning to move in together and everything. Alan has been introduced to Sonny's mum – she owns and runs a Chinese restaurant off Shaftesbury Avenue.'

'I did know that. What do you mean I don't notice things …?'

'You're hopeless. Anyway, Sonny's lovely Mummy likes him and approves of him because he's bright apparently, though not as clever as Sonny I think, so they are both allowed to move into the flat, which has a spare bedsit area since their last lodger died in a shoot-out.'

'A shoot-out?! Stop! *What?*'

'This is Soho, you know,' says Ricci, lightly 'Never a dull moment. Who knows the details? Who even cares? That's all history. The important thing is that Sonny and dear Alan are together. The kids in First Aid have noticed and it's made them very excitable. Have you got our tickets for Joseph, by the way? I'm really looking forward to that.'

'Yes, but hang on. Mrs Oppah *nursing?*'

'Yes! It's adorable. Apparently, all this first aid has been her inspiration. She was training to be a nurse before she got married, way back when she was eighteen, but when she met Mr Oppah and got married, she had to give it all up. When he ran off with the lady in the next door flat she thought about applying again, but felt the children were too small to be left. Well, not small in Ali's case obviously – young, too young to be left. Now she feels the time has come. Jai and Sheena agree and have hastened her on the path. I helped her fill in the person specification for her interview earlier.'

'That's so good. I wondered if Jai might become a nurse...'

'Doctor. Jai doesn't want to become a "fucking nurse" because...'.

He waves his fingers to indicate Jai's inverted commas;

'all you do all day is...'

'Clear up shit?'

'Yep. You guessed it.'

'I didn't know Mrs Oppah's husband ran off with the lady next door.'

And on we chatter, until Nelly gets restless and begins to whine politely.

'Can she hear Glory and Sally do you suppose?'

'Of course, but also she's hungry, aren't you darling girl? Needs her tea. And so do your brood and that nice man, or do they get their own? You're no cook, are you? Has he still got his beard?'

'He's twizzled it down to a Freudian point and a twirly moustache. I think he may be a bit bored, Ricci.'

I'm a trifle hurt that Ricci has seen fit to criticise first my powers of observation and now my cooking, but he is right, I suppose. I had no idea about Sonny and Alan and I have no idea what supper will be.

'Ah, we're all bored, aren't we all? It's the lot of the middle aged man. But somehow Sylvie, I feel more positive about our future at the moment. Something has lifted or shifted. Do you feel it too? Nelly does.'

Nelly just looks hungry.

'It's been great getting you more involved with school nursing. Maybe you're on the change, coming over to the dark side…?!'

'Maybe, who knows. I should ask the ghosts. See what they have to say. Oh and have you heard Theo's news, talking of supernatural beings?'

'No. I don't notice things, remember.'

'So true, so true. Oh well, the grapevine is buzzing with this one. Can a grapevine buzz? Theo's leaving. He's off to heavenly pastures new, our God is. I'm surprised he hasn't told you. Come on Nelly dear, home time.'

And with one leap across the hall he is off and out, scooping up Nelly as he goes, the big brown door swinging shut behind them.

I am left alone in our hall, where we never feel completely alone.

'Glory? Sally?' The voices of those who have died are quiet this evening. I notice the blue and green tiles have a pattern of intertwining grapevine and one little bird in a branch. Who says I don't notice things? I noticed the detail on these tiles, I noticed a goose in the tree.

Ah. But a lot passes you by, Mum. Ricci's right.

Does it? Theo is leaving and I think I might mind about that. It feels like a loss.

We are all still here, if you need us to be.

But no one says that. That is what I would have liked to hear in my head as though Theo were talking, or on the imaginary breeze that sometimes blows through this hall. Nothing this evening. And Finn has gone quiet too. Time to go home.

Chapter Fourteen

'Hello, hello dears, here are our tickets. Sylvie, Alan, Sonny, Molly, Grace and Olly… so exciting. I'm just thrilled Mr Simpson has allowed the whole team to come. Girls, Olly and Alan - we are going to *love* this.

We are gathered outside the school, Ricci dressed what can really be best described as a technicolor dream coat.

'Great jacket, Ricci.'

Nelly wears a matching one, tied with ribbons under her tummy.

'Do you like it, Sylvie? I won't upstage Joseph, will I? God, I adore school plays. Do you remember the thrill of it all, Grace dear, Molly?'

One of them mumbles about it being a long time back. In fact I doubt either will hear much, but they both look pleased to be here. They've both entered into the spirit of technicolor, with Molly in flares and a cheesecloth blouse, Grace in a purple kaftan. The evening is warm, there is summer on the breeze.

Alan and Sonny look very loved up. No one could fail to notice now. Arms linked, they are pouring over the poster slapped up on the outside wall of school, pointing out the names of the children they know, which by now is pretty much all of them.

'It's only a Year Six production, Ricci. Don't get your hopes too high.'

'How could it not be good, in the shadow of theatre-land, a stones-throw from such thespian haunts as – what's the theatre opposite called?'

'The Windmill,' pipes up Molly.

'Oh, good Lord, is it? 'He squints across the road

'Yes, you're right. The Windmill. Famous theatre, tableaux vivant and now… International Table Dance Club. Oh.'

'It has a long and illustrious history,' says Molly.

'Of sorts,' says Grace.

'Come on, let's go in,' says Ricci, ever-bright, then stopping abruptly to read the inscription above the door;

''The fear of the Lord is the beginning of wisdom', my thoughts exactly" he chuckles.

Joseph dazzles. Clever Will Simpson has found the school an excellent music teacher, who also works at The Coliseum in St Martin's Lane and raises their Year Six game to great heights, as well as bringing in a professional band to accompany them, for a very small fee. This is one of the advantages of having your primary school situated in the heart of our capital. And, of course, we are all besotted with Year Six anyway, so we're predisposed to enjoy. Naturally every parent or carer is here, squashed into the completely unfit for purpose, but imaginatively adapted, school hall. And every single child has a part, even if it is a singing sheaf of corn or sack of grain. Ricci is rapt, Molly and Grace, who remember the original productions in the 1970s at the Westminster Theatre no doubt, tap their platform heeled feet and hum along.

Ali Oppah is a commanding Pharaoh, Bailey a convincingly mean brother and Pearl, miraculously restored to health, wellbeing and more besides, holds us all in her thrall. She leaps, she sings, she acts and we are completely under her spell when she calls to her hapless Joseph, with a maturity beyond her years: 'Come and lie with me, love!'

'I told you that kid could act,' whispers Will Simpson.

168

'Yes, a transformation. But who is Joseph? I don't think I know that boy, do I? He's as good as any of the choir boys at the Abbey.'

'He's a she. That's Kayleigh, of course! Great, isn't she?'

Kayleigh has us all in tears with 'Close every door to me', and as the makeshift curtain falls and rises and falls and rises many times (because there really is nothing like a school production when we all know and love every performer), she runs to give her flowers to a very slim, decorous woman sitting on the front row, who is clapping more happily than anyone.

'That's her mum,' shouts Sonny to me, over the applause. 'Kayleigh will be so happy her mum came.'

Afterward, I join the queue of parents congratulating Kayleigh's mum on her talented girl. Up close, Kayleigh's mum looks intractably tired, but she is still smiling;

'Good, ain't she? She loves that first aid you and Dr Ricci do, nurse, so thanks for that. Its taught her a lot. For a while she wanted to be a doctor an' all, but I'm hoping now she'll achieve the ambition I never and make a career on the stage.'

'Were you an actress?'

'Used to be an exotic dancer, but it all went tits up along the way. We've got to make sure that don't happen to Kayleigh, eh?'

'She can really sing, too, can't she?'

'Yeah. Her dad was a musician, I think.'

Kayleigh comes up to hug her mum and beam at us all, as we stand admiring her. She still has her stage makeup on and with her new gamine haircut, looks startlingly graceful and shining, with new assurance.

They all come up after that, as the after-party gets underway, with Mars Bars and Fanta for the kids, wine for their parents and guests, Ali waddling over in his Pharaoh costume and Bailey with his arm around Pearl, breathless from her exertions,

I smile at her and we all praise her for her acting.

Bailey is hugging Kayleigh's mum too now. She grins at me, ruffling his scruffy hair.

'His mum was my best mate. Good kid.'

And I'm reassured to see a couple who must be Bailey's foster carers hovering with his normal clothes, for changing into. They too are grinning proudly and entering into the festivities, but they look sensible and strong. They would give off the right, 'don't mess with us' message to any gang member, so we can hope Bailey is safe, for now.

'Oh my darling dears, who would have *thought* you could be such great actors as well as paramedics par-excellence? Thank you so much for this evening. Thank you thank you!' says Ricci,

'Now, see you all tomorrow, at First Aid. No excuses, just because you're stage struck. We have a very special visitor coming.'

We all troop out onto the street and say our happy goodbyes. Night time in Soho now and another world is waking up. I walk home through the park and I am just reaching goose-nest tree when a text from Finn comes through.

Hey, Sylvie. Hope Joseph was good. Guess who turned up at the café today?

Tell…

Crocus Lettison, art teacher of old!

No!

She was sweet. Hardly changed, tad more wrinkly.

Blue smock, bulb-like appearance, drop on nose?

Yes to all. Gentle manner though. And she is asking to rent a space in the upper room of the pavilion! Mingling of worlds old and new, eh? And will give the café artistic clout...she sure could draw!

***

We have arranged that I start our First Aid session today. Ricci is going to come out with Tony the paramedic in a bit and bring the long-awaited practice defibrillator, but this is to be a surprise for the class. Also today we are half expecting our visitation from The Powers, but having been initially so keen to inspect us, they have had to postpone a few weeks due to important meetings and lately have gone rather quiet. I had a provisional date from one of them for this week, but we won't be holding our collective breath waiting for them today. There are rumblings of shake-ups on high and whilst it's a community nurse's nature to grumble about our bosses, we know we are lucky we don't have to do their wearying jobs, but can instead teach children on the grass in the sun.

Alan and Sonny are setting up the food table with Mrs Oppah and Sonny's mother. The humble squash and biscuits we began with back at the start of term are history now and ever more elaborate treats appear, to the delight of the children. Mrs Oppah and Sonny's mum vie for superiority, plying the table with buns galore. Sonny has a deal going with the EAT in the corner of the square, so that we get all their left over sandwiches and sometimes Ana's chef comes by with a big bowl of chips. Its established that Rejoice and the McDougals take priority in collecting up the leftovers to take home at the end.

'It's really more picnic than First Aid now, isn't it?' says Alan.

'Well that's probably meeting a social outcome and perfectly measurable too, don't you think?'

'I'm not sure the Powers will see it that way.'

'Never mind. Now, today we're going to recap on burns.'

'Burns, not buns,' smiles Alan.

'Boor-ing'.

'Not boring. Very important. You could save a life, but you could also greatly minimise a person's discomfort and maintain calm if you get the first aid for burns right, so let's see who remembers?'

'Cold running water for a minimum of ten minutes. No toothpaste, no ice, no bowl of water because it warms up as the heat comes off the burn. See. Easy effing peesy!' says Jai.

'Not so fast. I mean, you are right, but...'

'I thought you was bringing the effing AED today.'

Effing is better than fucking, I note, but don't say.

'Aha, yes, lets properly recap on burns for twenty minutes and then there might be a defib surprise. How about a scenario to get us started?'

They leap up and start to arrange themselves into their natural groups. Phil, Rejoice and Ana are late and are only now coming across the grass, laughing together, pointing in the direction of Ana's chef's restaurant. Good of them to come at all when they have exams. Lloyd has spread out the baby Annies on a blanket under his mum's picnic table and is feeding them small triangles of samosa.

'We have fun here Sylvie, innit?' says Kayleigh, snuggling up to me with uncharacteristic affection. She is pretty in an impish way, with her new hair and hasn't managed to rub off all her eye make-up.

'You look like Twiggy.'

'Yeah, me mum said that, an' all. Did you like her?'

'Your mum? Very much. She was so proud of you. We all were. I just didn't know you could sing.'

'And you didn't expect Pearl to dance, neither, I bet. Whatever next, eh?'

'Are you both going to Langham Girls next term.'

'Yeah, course. But Bailey's going to a weird school with yellow socks. I'll miss him.'

'But he'll be safe.'

Kayleigh puts her hand up to her cheek, as thought to fiddle with a plait

'Oh, I keep doing that!' But then she nods vigorously

'Me and Ali knew he weren't okay, but we couldn't tell no one.'

'I know, Kayleigh, but you should always feel able to tell us, or your mum, or Mr Simpson…'.

'Not always. You just can't, Sylvie. You don't get it. Oi, Ali, you fat pig. Can you be my burns victim?'

Ali turns round to face us, with a beatific smile.

And then there isn't even a bang. A thud. A heavy thud in the solar plexus, then a soft, terrifying cloud of silence like a huge white cot blanket spreading tenderly over us all. I look around me, up from the grass where I have landed and feel a tender sorrow for us all, as though we were all precious patients up in the sunny ward, back in the day when there used to be patients in wards in this place. Soft, snowy ash is falling on us all, like a nineteen sixties song in our Soho Square, our precious old square. Like an old song that we are all gently singing, a song of silence.

So, this has happened…

173

... and I try to speak, but no sounds. No one is making any sounds.

I see Kayleigh rubbing her eyes like a tired, puzzled baby in a completely different part of the park from me. She had been by my side. I see Cynthia McDougal huddled with Sidney and Lloyd, shaking together under Shakespeare's house. Buns are strewn everywhere and the table has collapsed. One of the manikins has been blown into a tree and Ali sits awkwardly underneath, propped against the trunk.

Other park dwellers seem to be lying about randomly and for some more seconds very few people are moving.

I can't see all the children. Where are they? What happened to Rejoice, Phil and Ana who were walking towards us by the railing? Where are Sonny and Alan?

We are all slow motion, like a film is, like they say it is.

Like they say what is? What has happened?

Then Tony the paramedic and Ricci are coming out, rushing onto the square. We are a speeded up film now. Action is happening. I can't move to reach them.

Hello

I can't be heard.

What is the word I need, even? It isn't hello.

I try to wave, but my arms don't move yet.

Help.

Theo?

Help is the word you can't say.

Oh yes. That's right. Help. Help us please.

174

There is another person moving over the grass, conferring with Ricci. I recognise her as a highly appointed member of The Powers That Be, the one who had promised to visit us. She has picked an inconvenient time. We are not at our best just now. I hope Ricci will explain. She looks nice. And competent. She looks like an old fashioned nurse in a crisis, who will help take control and lead us all up to the wards.

I see Jai picking her way through the square, scrutinising the people who lie in the grass.

Danger, Response, Airway, Breathing... Danger

Remember it means Danger to yourself first, Jai. Is there any danger to you?

But Jai is fearless and dismissive of danger to herself. She is moving to administer first aid to others, as she has been trained.

Cometh the hour, cometh Jai.

And cometh Rejoice and Ana and Phil. And Ashley and Sheena and ... everyone is standing up or coming over and beginning to move about the casualties.

Casualties, as though it is an emergency.

It is an emergency, Sylvie.

So it is. An emergency is emerging.

Some of us seem to be unable to move, like a bad dream, but others of us move freely. Ali is stuck under his tree. The manikins are tossed all about, like the buns. I spot a Baby Annie on Shakespeare's roof. I feel very strange, stuck here on my patch of grass, unable to panic properly, proud of my charges. My heart is full of love, boundless, bounding love, I think. My heart is bounding.

175

Will you look at them? Wonderful, aren't they? You have trained them well, you and Ricci.

Glory? Is that you?

Yes dear, of course. Sssh now...they are on their way to you. You rest here.

I see Glory moving among the wounded people, helping and caring, wearing the normal old corduroy skirt she used to wear to work. I see Kayleigh jumping up and down frantically by someone who is lying down. Ricci and Tony running to her with a stretcher, moving a limp boy onto the stretcher very tenderly, Glory kneeling by his head, stroking his face. Plank.

Plank! Plank is not okay.

Quietly, Sylvie. You should close your eyes for a while now.

Sally? You here too?

Trust us, Sylvie. Close your eyes.

Trust. Trust the Trust. That's funny. Two meanings for the same word. Or is it the same word? NHS trust, trust the NHS...

And I close my eyes for a moment against the blue flashing that has started up, all over the square. Ambulance blue, emergency blue.

***

They are bringing us away from the square and through the door to our hall now. Our green and pleasant entrance hall or exit hall. A place of coming and going and resting and waiting. A place that is on the way to the sunny, healing wards above.

Those wards were closed long ago, stupid.

They were, of course. Very stupid of me. There are empty, carpeted rooms upstairs waiting for corporate occupation that hasn't yet arrived. Empty space. No wards. Pity. Wards would have been useful today.

I am on a little stretcher bed in the hall, by the indoor palm and the confidential waste bin. I am not hurt, so there is no need for me to be lying here, but here I lie. Glory passes by.

Glory, why am I on a stretcher? I am not hurt. Plank. Plank was hurt.

Plank is with us dear, we are looking after Plank.

Trust us, Sylvie.

Only that is not quite right, because Glory has died. Glory and Sally have died already. Plank is with us in the land of the living, not with them, beyond the veil. I should remind them, politely.

I see everyone moving round Plank's little stretcher bed. Kayleigh and Ricci and Tony the paramedic. Philomena is holding open the door of the hall, Jai is holding a defibrillator and together they open it on the floor, kneeling by Plank.

Don't practice on each other, Jai. That would be very dangerous, remember.

They're not practising, dear.

Glory?

Close your eyes and rest, Sylvie. Trust us, all shall be well

Sally?

Sally has told me that all shall be well, as Mother Julian of Norwich was wont to say. All shall be well and all shall be well and all manner of things shall be well. I trust the warm and welcoming green tiled hall and the good people passing through, but I am very much unsure that all shall be well.

Oh, Theo here too? Yes, Theo, I know. That was what Mother Julian wrote. It is often quoted.

There was more, Sylvie. A bit we often miss out.

Theo, I don't think I have time for quotation and speculation just now. You see, there is an emergency emerging and we are all extremely busy here in the hall as you see, some arriving, some leaving.

Just saying, Sylvie.

I can't seem to help them with Plank. I notice with pride that Philomena is doing a magnificent job of triaging at the door, Jai is learning from Toni how to defibrillate and Kayleigh is stroking Plank's face tenderly, as Glory has shown her, though I don't think Kayleigh has noticed Glory. Ricci says I am unnoticing, but I find myself quite otherwise. Everyone stands back and I notice they are shocking Plank. Tony is in command, Jai at his right hand. Every person's face is pale. People with dark skin go just as pale as white skinned people when they are worried sick, I notice. My heart is bounding in my head, pounding.

They shock Plank another time. I feel frightened for Plank and suddenly very cold.

Close your eyes and rest, Sylvie.

And I don't want to shut my eyes, though I am grateful to Sally for being with me when there is so much else to do, but my eyes seem to be closing anyway. I force them to open and I see them gently pulling a red blanket up and over Plank, covering his lovely face.

Oh...

My heart is bounding with love for them all, though I cannot reach them to say. No fear, not frightened now, but pity and bounding love.

This bit.

Theo?

This bit, Sylvie. Listen. Mother Julian also added this bit: 'For there is a force of love moving through the universe that holds us fast and will never let us go.'

Oh, that bit. Thank you, Theo.

Comforting?

Soothing, even.

And I close my eyes.

Chapter Fifteen

I watch Ricci's mouth carefully as he speaks. Something like: 'Silent contemplation.'

'I know. I always coveted the contemplative life.'

'How have six weeks of silence felt?'

'Cut off.'

'Contemplative?'

'A bit, maybe.'

Ricci nods. We are having good strong coffee at Finn's prime table, looking out to sea. He has come up to Cromer for the weekend to visit, bringing Nelly, who is sitting politely as ever, but probably longs to get out onto the beach with a stick.

Kayleigh and Bailey are making an elaborate sandcastle, down below on the beach, with Sonny and Alan supervising their endeavours.

Everyone has come up this summer, staying with kind Cromer families, who have been moved by their story. The bomb blast had made national headlines, of course; for the inevitable damage and casualty caused, but also for the bravery and competence (yes, that word) of our First Aid children. TV footage of the immediate aftermath, showed unusually small people moving around the disaster scene, applying direct pressure to bleeding wounds, directing firemen to get water onto burns, rolling unconscious patients into the recovery position and so on.

As soon as the full force of the official emergency service had appeared, the children were picked off and taken to the nearest hospital, being almost all to some degree injured or shocked themselves. But considering the volume of explosive and proximity to the site, most of our injuries had been surprisingly minimal and the First Aid was agreed to be of the highest standard. Had they not been protected by our Trust (in which we had found new trust) and by the likes of Will Simpson and Alice as a firm firewall, they would have been exploited as mini celebrities.

It had not been the terrorist attack we all half-anticipate every working day in London, but a rogue SC 250 left over from the Blitz and unearthed by the high speed railway tunneling machinery, yards from Soho Square. A fluke bomb, an abhoration… is that a word?

A fund had been started by Finn's community café folk and unlikely links between Soho and Cromer had begun to form; Alan and Sonny, coming up to visit me, had been so taken by the town and by the low property prices, that they had begun to make plans to settle here and investigate school nursing options in Norfolk.

Kayleigh's face had become poster famous, after an unscrupulous snap of her sitting on clinic steps, shortly after Plank had been taken away. Her eyes, still ringed with stage makeup from the previous evening, were lifted directly to camera in sorrow and shock. This photograph moved members of the general public to donate wildly to the fund and somehow the idea of summer recuperation in Cromer became a viable reality, as guest houses and hotels made rooms available. Kayleigh and her mum, Bailey and his foster carers are VIP guests of The Hotel de Paris, for as long as they care to stay.

'You can never be sure how a blast wave will travel.'

Tony the paramedic had explained to me afterwards, as I sat up in my hospital bed. This one seems to have been predictably random. Your injuries are classic; primary injury from barotrauma, from an initial blast wave impacting on your body.'

At that stage I had needed Tony and everyone else to write everything down as I couldn't hear and was useless at lip-reading. The doctors had written 'Tympanic membrane perforation (TM). Possible ossicular separation in addition, resulting in conductive hearing loss. Possibly also damaged cochlea.'

Tony explained painstakingly that TM is considered a physical marker of significant blast exposure. He underlined 'Significant', because I seemed to have difficulty taking in the idea that my injuries weren't superficial.

'Also concussion. You may experience confusion, hear voices in your head.'

'But I didn't bang my head.'

'No visible signs of head injury, but extreme positive-pressure waves may cause the brain to move inside the skull, resulting in brain injury, mild to severe.'

'And mine is mild?'

'Yes, probably but still significant. More tests to come, Sylvie. You must be a properly patient patient.'

'I don't feel confused.'

When I wrote this or tried to tell people, I noticed that they would smile politely, kindly, even quite patronisingly. I decided to keep quiet about the voices in my head.

'My head does bound a bit. I mean pound.'

'You need to rest it, keep your eyes closed,' Tony said.

But whenever I closed my eyes, I would remember Sally's gentle instruction and experience the same fright and coldness as I had in the hall. Our lovely hall, where people came and went. I would forget and then I would remember again

'Plank.'

'Plank died, Sylvie.'

'I know. I know.'

I could lip-read that one, but Tony wrote it down anyway, so I didn't forget again. His clinical explanations helped and I kept the notes he wrote until they were tatty scraps, referring to them again and again, as facts drifted in and out of my brain.

'Plank died of "blast lung"; severe pulmonary contusion, bleeding or swelling with damage to alveoli and blood vessels – most common cause of death, from blast overpressures, or shock waves.'

'His lungs were never very strong. His poor family.'

Tony has neat, small writing. I speak back, but can't hear my own voice, so am uncertain how clear I am making myself.

'I know. I know. Cynthia, Angus, Sidney and Lloyd were shaken but otherwise completely unharmed by the blast, thank God. And the council have taken pity and are moving them into the Berwick Street Buildings; into the Oppah flat actually.'

'Where are the Oppah family going?'

'Ground floor. The children are all such local heroes; the council is bending over backwards to support them. Did you hear Ali broke his leg again? The poor kid. Almost funny, that. And hey presto! Four-bedroom flat on the ground floor, no lift, now.'

I remember Ali slumped against the tree, rubbing his head like a puzzled bear, the manikin stuck above him in the branches.

'Poor Ali.'

'Sylvie, it could have been so much worse.'

'Plank died.'

'But Sylvie.' Tony reaches over and pats my hand, then writes.

'Plank was the only fatality. The only one. From a 1000lb bomb. In large part that was luck, because the blast waves seem to have torn down an alleyway, past the Catholic church, missing buildings, but everyone acknowledges that your kids and their amazing first aid made a big difference.'

'With the secondary injuries?'

'Yes, exactly.' Tony is very patient with his writing

'Penetrating wounds or blunt trauma caused by flying debris. The kids looked after the general public. Proper *FIRST* aid, not like we paramedics, who are Second Aid, of course.'

I had smiled reading this.

'First Aid, not Second Aid. That's what we used to tell them.'

***

After hospital time, my patient family moved me up to Cromer like an invalid of old. Cromer, the last resort, as it was known in the nineteen hundreds. Salubrious Cromer for people who couldn't afford the more exclusive rest cures of Baden Baden in Germany.

It had been nearly summer holiday time when the bomb happened.

Now we are in high summer. The light today is artist's light, so strong you notice everything. I watch Ricci's face closely, as he speaks, noticing that he looks older and wearier, despite his sun browned face. Since I haven't been hearing so well, I notice more, or fancy I do.

'I'm not going back, Sylvie.'

'I don't mean to be dramatic Ricci, but is there anything to go back to?'

'Oh, the building was fine, blast damage to some trees in the square and lots of tiles off from Oxford Street to Tottenham Court Road, but nothing major.'

'I didn't mean the building.'

'No, well Molly and Grace were planning to retire anyway and with Alan and Sonny looking to move up here when they qualify, we wouldn't be much of a team. The Powers have decided to close our 'Soho outpost' as they call it – ironic, when we thought Soho was the centre – and "reintegrate" us into one of the larger teams. Lovely Olly will be fine wherever he goes, an asset to any team.'

Ricci sees my stricken face

'It might not be such a bad thing, Sylvie. Our practice was becoming increasingly idiosyncratic, don't you think?'

'I loved our team.'

'I know. Me too. But it is time to change and move on. What was it Kotter the management guru said; "turbulence will never cease"?'

We look at the rolling sea.

'Oh and Theo will have left now, won't he?'

Theo had written me a letter. Old fashioned to get a letter, but it had seemed entirely appropriate, as I had sat on the pavilion, in my silent world. Finn had even found an old wicker bath chair in the pavilion store room. Crocus Lettison the art teacher had restored it in duck-egg blue, stating firmly, but kindly: 'Convalescence is an old fashioned concept, demanding an old fashioned chair.'

'The silence has been quite welcome at times Ricci, for thinking it all through, you know?'

'Such as?'

'School nursing. Where it fits, what it means'

'And your conclusions?'

'None yet. I just keep coming back to Plank and the importance of being there, alongside children and young people. We don't know how long their lives or ours will be. It isn't always about preparing them for being grownups.'

'But for being alongside them now.'

'Yes.'

I still hear Theo in my head sometimes, offering useful advice

These are your own thoughts, Sylvie, not mine.

I know Theo. But I listen better when they seem to come from you.

I don't hear Sally or Glory. They have gone now.

Ricci strokes Nelly's soft neck.

'And you will take all that with you wherever you go in the autumn, Sylvie. School nursing doesn't have to be one place or one way, you know that. There are many school worlds, that's what you always said. School nursing is wherever the children are. Come on Nelly. You need a run and I need to see what those naughty children have been making on the beach. Did you hear that Kayleigh and Bailey made a nude woman for the sandcastle competition, complete with seaweed in all the hairy places.'

'Brilliant. Did they win?'

'Disqualified, until the judges recognised Kayleigh and then they got a consolation prize. Great here, isn't it?'

'Yes. Did you know Philomena, Rejoice and Ana are coming up this weekend on the train? They're bringing Phil's mum.'

'Cool. Who's bringing them?'

'They're coming on their own, pretty much, but I gather head mistress Alice is seeing them as far as Norwich. She is off back to King Street to revisit Mother Julian.'

'And I bumped into Mrs Oppah in Budgen's. The family that own the guest house on the Front have taken them in for the whole summer, funded by the fund, who have also bought Ali a brand new whizzy wheelchair. I can't believe that poor kid broke his leg again.'

'He's taking it as stoically as ever. And he is getting daily physio up at Cromer hospital, so he should be fine by the autumn.'

Finn comes over.

'More coffee you two?'

'Not for me, darling heart, I'm off down to the sea again, to the lonely sea and the sky, if only! Laters.'

Finn sits down.

'Well I've brought Sylvie the latest bun. Sonny's mum has been teaching us how to make Mooncakes in the kitchen. They are incredibly fiddly, layer upon layer, like sandstone cliffs.'

'Mooncakes are not buns. Small, flat bottom, remember.'

'Yes, fair point. And I'll sit down for a minute. We've been so busy today.'

'You're busy every day, Finn.'

The pavilion project has expanded exponentially and the local council is all smiles, but the café rota detail has yet to be ironed out. Our own children have been helping willingly, but sporadically. Finn bears the brunt, but she looks very well on it, I notice, with my newly found gift for noticing. She looks strong and enviably slim and happy. I notice she doesn't have much time to eat the buns herself.

Finn is also easy to hear, maybe because she has that gift of giving everyone she speaks to her full attention.

'I'm fine.' She smiles: 'I get my sacred two hours' peace in the pavilion every morning. That's perfect for now. No fretting on my behalf. I suppose your book kind of finished itself, story-wise, didn't it?'

'Kind of.'

Finn wipes her hands on her floral pinny.

'I came out to tell you that I have heard from Cynthia and Harold.'

As coordinator of the Fund, Finn has been in contact with the McDougals, on and off all summer.

'Good news. A lovely little cottage has come free, just up by the lighthouse, near Happy Valley. The owners are going to Spain for a fortnight and have offered it up for Plank's family. I spoke to Cynthia this morning and they are planning to arrive tomorrow. The weather is set fair until the end of the month Sylvie. I know it's no consolation, the smallest gesture, but…'.

'It's so kind. Thank you, Finn. How did Cynthia seem?'

Finn's eyes meet mine and we are for a moment every mother, contemplating the unthinkable loss of a child. There are no words, so we just look out to sea for a bit.

After a minute, Finn gets up. "Better get on, Sylvie. But one very good thing. The council and committee have unanimously agreed on a name for the café. North Wind Pavilion Community Arts Café was too much of a mouthful.'

'What have they decided?'

Finn spreads her arms our wide, laughing;

'Well, I'm sure you'll agree that what we have here is a bohemian hub, a thriving, artisan centre of creativity and celebration of diversity, where all are welcome, where all may thrive.'

'We do.'

'We brought our worlds together, Sylvie. Look.'

She points me over to the pavilion, where two volunteers are knocking in a new wooden panel above the door. It reads: Soho on Sea.'

The End

Printed in Great Britain
by Amazon

79198876R00109